"I've done nothing I need be ashamed of!"

Jennifer's hazel eyes flashed as she spat the words at the man confronting her.

"I know Mike's reputation for seduction!" Hunter countered. "And besides, women lie so convincingly."

"You wouldn't know the truth if it hit you in the face!" Jennifer retorted.

The next instant she found herself crushed against his chest as his lips took hungry possession of her own. For turbulent minutes she was drowning in heady sensations. Then Hunter was holding her at arm's length.

"Do you usually allow a man such freedom, Miss Casey," he asked calmly, "or didn't Mike satisfy you entirely this evening?"

Without thinking Jennifer raised her hand and slapped him—hard. She wouldn't take Hunter's insults, even though she loved him.

YVONNE WHITTAL
is also the author of these
Harlequin Romances

and this

Harlequin Presents

Many of these titles are available at your local bookseller.

For a free catalogue listing all available Harlequin Romances
and Harlequin Presents, send your name and address to:

HARLEQUIN READER SERVICE,
1440 South Priest Drive, Tempe, AZ 85281
Canadian address: Stratford, Ontario N5A 6W2

The Spotted Plume

by

YVONNE WHITTAL

Harlequin Books

TORONTO • LONDON • LOS ANGELES • AMSTERDAM
SYDNEY • HAMBURG • PARIS • STOCKHOLM • ATHENS • TOKYO

Original hardcover edition published in 1981
by Mills & Boon Limited

ISBN 0-373-02478-9

Harlequin edition published May 1982

CHAPTER ONE

JENNIFER CASEY'S step was light but firm as she approached the Matron's office. It had taken her six long months to come to a decision about her future, and she was not going to be persuaded to change her mind, not even by Matron Griffiths whom she admired and respected.

Since Colin Ashton's death in a light aircraft accident, her life had had no meaning, and she had carried out her duties without her usual enthusiasm. She could see him now, his sandy-coloured hair lying in an unruly fashion across his forehead, and his white coat flapping about his legs as he strode through the hospital on his daily rounds. The memory still had the power to hurt with incredible fierceness, and she had to get away, for the simple reason that she could no longer remain where the past continued to haunt her. She had tried to face it in an effort to overcome the pain of her loss, but there were too many things in this hospital to remind her of the happiness they had shared, and the plans they had made for a future together.

The door to Matron's office stood open, but even though she was expected Jennifer knocked.

'Come in, Sister Casey, and close the door behind you.'

Matron Griffiths pushed aside the papers before her to look up at the fair, slim young woman standing tall and erect on the other side of her desk. She had known of Jennifer Casey's engagement to Dr Ashton before his tragic death, and she was aware, too, of the unhappiness which still lurked behind that composed exterior of one of her most competent senior nurses.

'I have received your resignation, Sister Casey,' she said in her quiet but authoritative voice, 'and I must ask you to reconsider.'

Those hazel eyes flecked with gold did not waver. 'I'm sorry, Matron, but I've made my decision.'

'I presume you have given this a great deal of thought?'

'I have, Matron.'

'Have you found yourself a post elsewhere?'

'Not yet,' Jennifer confessed. 'I have a little money saved, and I thought of spending a few weeks with my sister in Johannesburg before deciding on the future.'

Matron Griffiths frowned down at her desk. 'I'm not at all anxious to lose your services, Sister Casey, and I wonder if you would consider the proposition I'm about to put to you.' She drummed her fingers on the desk blotter, a sure sign that she was troubled. 'My sister, Alice Maynard, injured her hip some weeks ago, but she will be discharged from hospital and allowed to return home only on condition that she acquires the services of a qualified nurse. She lives on a farm in the Oudtshoorn district, which will give you the opportunity to get right away from Cape Town for a while, and, with only one patient to take care of, you will have plenty of time to enjoy the scenery.'

What Matron Griffiths was suggesting sounded tempting, but it would plunge Jennifer's plans into a state of total disarray. 'I—I don't know, Matron. I was——'

'Think it over and give me your answer tomorrow,' Matron interrupted amiably. 'If you agree, then I shall release you within seven days on extended, unpaid leave, and I'm hoping that while you're at Vogelsvlei you might think differently about resigning from here.'

'Vogelsvlei?' Jennifer questioned with some amusement. 'That's Dutch for Bird Valley,' Matron explained unnecessarily. 'My nephew farms there with ostriches, as most farmers do in the Oudtshoorn district, and if you haven't yet been that way, then you might find it extremely interesting and enlightening.' Her glance sharpened as it met Jennifer's. 'May I count on you to give my suggestion your most serious consideration?'

Jennifer hesitated, but only briefly. It could do no harm to consider the post which was being offered to her and, nodding slowly, she said: 'Yes, Matron, I'll consider it.'

'Good!' Matron Griffiths' voice was abrupt as she drew her papers towards her, signifying that their discussion was at an end. 'Come and see me again tomorrow.'

'Very well, Matron.'

In her rented, furnished flat, with its ever changing view of the Indian Ocean, Jennifer spent a restless night trying to decide what to do. She had made up her mind to leave the General Hospital, and possibly Cape Town as well, but she had never given a thought to private nursing, and most certainly not on an ostrich farm, of all places. She was tempted, she could not deny it, but private nursing was a highly specialised job, and one which she was not certain she would be able to cope with.

Matron Griffiths naturally hoped that, after a spell away from Cape Town, she would feel differently about returning to the General, but Jennifer had grave doubts about that. She had spent six months trying to shed her attachment to the shadow that followed her about, but she had been miserably unsuccessful. Colin was there in every corridor, and every ward, and the memory was a painful reminder of what might have been if fate had not stepped in so cruelly.

In Colin she had found the qualities she had searched for

in the man with whom she had felt she could spend the rest of her life. He had been kind, gentle, and dedicated, and she had grown to love and respect him for it. Now, at the age of twenty-four, she was preparing herself for a life dedicated to the service of others, for she was certain that no other man could take his place, nor touch her heart again in that special way.

There was no purpose in dwelling on the past; she had to think of the future, and perhaps Matron Griffiths' proposition was worth considering most carefully. A spell of private nursing could not harm her; it would, in fact, broaden her knowledge to prepare her for the future, whether it be at the General, or at a hospital elsewhere, and with this thought in mind she finally made a decision which was to affect her life in a way she had never dreamed of.

Things moved swiftly after Jennifer had informed Matron Griffiths of her willingness to accept the post she had offered her. She would be released from the General at the end of that week to begin her duties at Vogelsvlei on the following Monday at a salary which surpassed the one she was receiving at the hospital, and that was not something she could baulk at. Matron made all the necessary arrangements, and that left Jennifer with nothing more drastic to do than pay her flat rent a few months in advance, and to prepare herself for her trip to Oudtshoorn.

Jennifer received her final instructions from Matron Griffiths before leaving the General on the Saturday morning. If she left Cape Town early on the Monday morning she should reach Oudtshoorn round about lunch time, Matron calculated roughly, and Jennifer was to report to a Dr Tremayne at the Oudtshoorn hospital. Dr Tremayne, on her arrival, would give her further instructions with regard to the treatment he desired for his patient.

All other arrangements would be made from that end, Matron informed her and, rising from behind her desk, she extended her hand to clasp Jennifer's.

'Give my regards to my sister, and don't be intimidated by my nephew, Hunter. He's become a crusty old bachelor, and he's by nature an abrupt, often rude man, but you can rely on him to give you whatever assistance you may need.'

Jennifer drove away from the hospital with mixed feelings that morning. She was saying a temporary goodbye to a life she had known for some years, to venture out into a future which was still a mystery. She had no idea whether she was doing the right thing, but it was too late now to alter the course of events.

As Matron had suggested, Jennifer left Cape Town shortly before six o'clock on that cool September morning, and headed her white Fiat eastwards towards ostrich country. It was mid-morning when she stopped for tea at Swellendam, a picturesque town in the Bree Valley at the foot of the Langeberg range, and although she wished she could linger, she drank her tea quickly in order to resume her journey.

She had never travelled this way before, and the countryside enchanted her, most especially when she entered the fertile plain between the Swartberg and the forest-clad Outeniqua mountains. Fruit orchards and green fields of lucerne lay stretched out before her as she approached Oudtshoorn, and she succumbed to the temptation to stop and stare at the long-necked birds grazing in a field alongside the road. The ostrich's walk was ungainly on those two-toed feet which were so often mounted and sold as curios, but on its body it carried a fortune which had made

many a man wealthy during the ostrich-feather boom of
the early nineteen-hundreds, and many farmers had gone
bankrupt, too, when the market had slumped in 1914.

Oh, well! Jennifer sighed, pushing her fingers through
her shoulder-length hair which she had left free of its
customary confining knot. This was no time to day-dream
of that time when men made instant fortunes to build those
homesteads which were today referred to as 'Ostrich
Palaces.' Dr Tremayne was awaiting her arrival in the
hospital somewhere in Oudtshoorn, and she presumed that,
like most doctors, he hated being kept waiting.

She stopped at a filling station in Oudtshoorn to freshen
up in the cloakrooms, and after making the necessary
enquiries she drove directly to the hospital where Dr
Tremayne, a robust man in his fifties, ushered her into a
small office to explain the treatment he had prescribed for
his patient. 'So far, so good,' Jennifer decided when she
discovered that she was not expected to do anything she had
not done many times before. Ahead of her was still her
meeting with Alice Maynard and her son Hunter, and
Jennifer was not at all sure whether this encounter would
transpire as smoothly as the one with Dr Tremayne.

She was escorted up a flight of stairs and along a passage
to a private ward in that wing. The murmur of voices could
be heard behind the closed door, but Jennifer could never
explain afterwards exactly what her feelings had been at
that moment when Dr Tremayne pushed open the door
and stood aside for her to precede him into the room.

In a wheelchair beside the bed sat a grey-haired woman
with curiosity mirrored in her grey eyes, and a ready smile
on her lips, but it was the man leaning against the wall beside the window who drew Jennifer's attention and held it
for interminable, heart-stopping seconds.

Jennifer was tall, but this man was considerably taller, with dark hair brushed back severely from a broad forehead. His jaw was square with a hint of iron determination in its structure, and the wide, powerful shoulders tapered down to lean hips and long-limbed muscular legs clad in grey slacks of an expensive linen. It was not, however, his physical appearance that made her feel as if the air was being squeezed systematically from her lungs, but the intense ferocity in those deep blue eyes as they raked her dispassionately from head to foot until she felt stripped of the calmness and confidence which was so much a part of her nature.

'Who the devil is this?' he thundered in a deep voice that not only set her nerves quivering, but stirred up an antagonism which made her stiffen with dislike.

'Allow me to introduce Sister Jennifer Casey,' Dr Tremayne said at once. 'Matron Griffiths assured me telephonically that she's an excellent nurse, and I have no doubt at all that Mrs Maynard will be well taken care of.'

Hunter Maynard pushed himself away from the wall to lessen the distance between them, and the intimidating height and breadth of him made Jennifer wish herself anywhere but there at that moment.

'I was under the impression that my aunt was sending us an elderly nurse,' he announced harshly, transferring his ferocious gaze to Dr Tremayne, but it was Jennifer who replied.

'I'm certain your aunt never once mentioned my age.'

'You're damn right she didn't!' he barked, his incinerating glance sweeping over her once more and reducing her to the level of an incompetent child. 'If she had, you wouldn't be here now, I can assure you!'

'Now, Hunter, don't make such a fuss.' Alice Maynard

spoke for the first time, and her voice was pleasantly warm. 'I'm sure Sister Casey must be tired after her long journey, and we still have quite a distance to travel out to the farm.'

An antagonistic silence hovered in the room, then Hunter Maynard drew himself up to his full, imperious height and shot a glowering glance at the man standing beside Jennifer.

'Before we leave here I'd like a private word with you, Dr Tremayne.'

'Certainly, Mr Maynard,' Dr Tremayne said at once, and Jennifer experienced a certain amount of relief when she found herself alone with Mrs Maynard a few moments later.

'Don't pay too much attention to my son, Sister Casey,' she said apologetically with a glimmer of laughter in her eyes. 'He can be rather boorish at times, but his moods seldom last long.'

Jennifer was not concerned with Hunter Maynard's moods at that moment. She was convinced that he was doing his level best to have her taken off the case, and her future was suddenly plunged into a state of uncertainty.

'I'm sorry if I'm not what you expected, Mrs Maynard.'

'Don't be silly, my dear,' Alice Maynard waved aside Jennifer's remark. 'I'm sure we're going to get on very nicely together and, to be quite honest, I'm terribly relieved that my sergeant-major sister hasn't sent a replica of herself. I wouldn't have been able to bear it.'

Amusement lifted the corners of Jennifer's generous mouth. 'Matron Griffiths can be a terror at times, but at heart she's a warm and marvellously understanding person.'

'I know,' Alice Maynard admitted, her grey eyes twinkling mischievously, 'but I'm still very grateful that she had the sense to send someone like yourself.'

Their conversation ended abruptly when the door was wrenched open to admit a thunderous-looking Hunter Maynard, and Jennifer gathered at once from his expression that he had failed in his attempts to have her replaced.

'Are you ready, Mother?' he demanded abruptly.

'I've been ready for ages, as you very well know,' Alice Maynard announced with a hint of irritation in her voice.

'There's just one thing I'd like to make absolutely clear before we leave here, Sister Casey,' he said, turning on Jennifer to subject her to the full fury of his incredibly blue eyes. 'Your stay at Vogelsvlei will be for the sole purpose of seeing to my mother's needs, and if you had some idea of turning it into a paid holiday, then you might as well go right back where you came from, and now.'

'Hunter!' Alice Maynard's voice held a sharp reprimand.

'Stay out of this, Mother!' he ordered harshly. 'I'm paying her salary, and I demand the right to make a few stipulations.'

There was a brief, angry silence, then Jennifer said with as much dignity as she could muster, 'I understand perfectly, Mr Maynard, but I'm not in the habit of taking a holiday at someone else's expense. I'm here to work, and that's exactly what I shall be doing.'

Those furious eyes raked her up and down once more, then he nodded abruptly, and picked up his mother's suitcase, leaving Jennifer to wheel Mrs Maynard from the ward, and down the passage towards the lift.

It was a silent party of three who emerged from the hospital building some minutes later to cross the parking area towards a dusty four-wheel-drive truck parked close by. With the muscles rippling beneath his white, short-sleeved shirt, he transferred his mother from the wheelchair into the cabin of the truck, and after folding up the chair he lifted it on to the back where he had flung his mother's suitcase moments before.

'Where's your car?' he asked Jennifer abruptly, and when she pointed to it some distance away, he added: 'Follow me, and step on it. I haven't all day.'

Jennifer turned without a word. He was the rudest man she had ever had the misfortune to meet, she decided as she walked quickly to her car and unlocked the door on the driver's side. She had come into contact with many different types of men during the course of her career, but none of them, not even Colin, had ever succeeded in disturbing the surface of her calm in the way Hunter Maynard had done. Matron Griffiths had warned her of his rude, often abrupt manner, but she had somehow never imagined that it would be like this, Jennifer thought and, turning the key in the ignition, she was soon following close behind the dusty truck as it left the hospital grounds.

Hunter Maynard drove fast once they had left the town behind them, but Jennifer managed to keep up with him. It was when they turned off on to a dirt road, however, that she was forced to lag behind if she did not want to choke on the dust being kicked up by the truck. Ten minutes later she began to wonder whether the heat and the dust would ever end, but it was not long after that when she found herself following the truck through an arched gateway with the name 'Vogelsvlei' painted in large black letters against the whitewashed background.

The homestead, when it emerged through the plein and pepper trees, monentarily robbed her of breath. She was actually looking at one of the 'Ostrich Palaces' she had heard so much about, and it was a sight that filled her with a great deal of awe. The white, two-storied mansion had a gabled roof, and a trellised verandah running along three sides of the lower portion of the house, with a similar balcony on the upper section, and it was surrounded by a spacious garden with shrubs and palms bordering the smooth green lawns.

Hunter Maynard parked his truck on the gravel drive in front of the house while Jennifer left her Fiat beneath the shade of a large pepper tree. She climbed out and, moving with a fluid, unconscious grace, she hurried towards the truck to offer her assistance, but two serving women and a man were there before her, and from their jubilant expressions she gathered that they were thrilled at having their Oumies Maynard back in their midst.

The wheelchair was transferred with speed from the truck to the verandah, and it was carefully dusted before Hunter placed his mother in it.

'Let me introduce you,' Mrs Maynard said as Jennifer stepped on to the verandah, and she gestured towards the two women. 'This is Nellie, our cook, and this is Agnes who supervises the cleaning of the house and sees to our personal needs. And this,' she added, pointing to the man carrying her suitcase from the truck, 'is Danny. Danny is Hunter's right-hand man on the farm, and he can usually put his hand to anything else that needs to be done around the house.' Alice Maynard's smile embraced the three trusted servants. 'I'd like you to meet Sister Jennifer Casey. She's going to look after me for a while.'

Nellie, the buxom one of the two women, was the first to react with a smiling, '*Dag, Nonnie*', and the others swiftly followed suit.

'If you'll give Danny the keys to your car he'll park it in the garages at the back,' Hunter instructed Jennifer, then he turned to Agnes. 'Go with Danny, and take Sister Casey's luggage up to her room.'

Jennifer handed her keys to Danny as instructed and,

as the servants dispersed, Hunter led the way into the house.

Her eyes literally bulged at what she saw, and it was with the greatest difficulty that she controlled her features when Hunter Maynard happened to glance in her direction over one broad, forbidding shoulder. There were crystal chandeliers hanging from the high ceiling above her, and Persian rugs beneath her feet, and wherever she looked she glimpsed the polished wood of priceless antiques. A little beyond the staircase with its intricately carved wooden balustrade, Hunter led the way into what appeared to be a spacious bedroom with an adjoining bathroom, and here, too, wood and brass gleamed with a polished brightness, while the expensive rugs beneath her feet muted their footsteps and the squeal of the wheelchair's tyres.

'I've had the guest suite prepared for you, Mother,' Hunter said in a clipped voice as he turned towards the grey-haired woman in the chair. 'I hope you'll find it comfortable until such time as you're mobile enough to attempt the stairs.'

'That was very thoughtful of you, Hunter,' his mother smiled up at him, then sighed and clasped her hands together in her lap. 'Oh, it's good to be home again!'

'Is there anything else you might need before I leave you?'

'No, dear,' Mrs Maynard shook her head, 'but you might just ask Nellie to prepare a light lunch for Sister Casey.'

'That isn't necessary, Mrs Maynard,' Jennifer protested hastily, but the older woman gestured her to silence.

'Nonsense, child! Hunter and I had something to eat at the hospital, but that's no excuse for letting you go hungry.' She glanced up at Hunter. 'Will you speak to Nellie?'

'I'll arrange something,' he replied, turning towards the door, but when he reached it he glanced back over his shoulder, and his electrifying glance travelled over Jennifer once more. 'By the way, Sister Casey, your room is to the left at the top of the stairs, and it's the second door on your right. That button next to my mother's bed is connected to a buzzer which will ring in your room if she should ever need you during the night, and if there's anything else you wish to know, then I suggest you come to me directly.' Without waiting for her to reply, he turned back to his mother and said abruptly, 'I'll see you later.'

The door closed behind him the next instant, and as his heavy footsteps grew fainter down the short passage, Alice Maynard sighed audibly. 'I think I'd like to lie down for a while. That trip home has tired me out slightly.'

Using her good leg as leverage, Alice Maynard made it easy for Jennifer to transfer her from the chair to the bed, and after adjusting the pillows, she asked, 'Are you comfortable, Mrs Maynard?'

'Yes, thank you, Jennifer.' She looked up a little guiltily and smiled that warm, embracing smile. 'I may call you Jennifer, may I not? It's such a pretty name, and Sister Casey seems so frighteningly formal.'

'You may call me whatever you like, Mrs Maynard,' Jennifer assured her brightly.

'I think I like you, Jennifer,' the older woman sighed. 'Give me an hour, will you? Then you can come and help me into that infernal chair so that we can have tea on the verandah.'

'I'll be back in an hour, Mrs Maynard,' Jennifer promised, and after making quite sure that her patient was comfortable, she left the room and closed the door quietly behind her.

In the passage she encountered the buxom Nellie, who told her that her lunch would be served within a few minutes in the dining-room and, after taking directions from her,

Jennifer ventured upstairs in search of her bedroom.

She found it without difficulty, and she found, too, that her suitcases had been unpacked for her. She was delighted, also, to find that she had been given a room with double glass doors leading out on to the upstairs balcony, and when she opened them she discovered that she had a magnificent view out over the garden towards the fields beyond where the ostriches grazed. She would love to explore the farm, she decided, but there was no time for that now. She felt hot and sticky, and she could do with a change of clothing before she went down to the lunch Nellie was preparing for her.

Fifteen minutes later she went downstairs feeling cool and refreshed after a quick wash in the bathroom across the passage from her bedroom, and she had changed into a white cotton overall, with her honey-blonde hair tied up once more in a neat, serviceable chignon.

Lunch, in the dining-room with its polished oak table, was a salad with an array of cold meats, as well as a pot of tea, and it was only when Jennifer started eating that she realised how hungry she had actually been. A tranquil silence reigned, and while she ate she allowed her glance to slide over the paintings adorning the panelled walls. They were originals, and mostly landscapes, except for the portrait of a fierce-looking man seated astride a magnificent white stallion.

The eyes were a magnetic, masterful blue beneath fierce dark brows, and there was an unquestionable familiarity in the high-bridged nose and square, determined chin. The mouth, however, was thinner, less sensuous, but it was undeniably Hunter Maynard's father, she decided when she noticed the proud, faintly arrogant tilt of the head, and the broad, powerful shoulders beneath the black riding jacket.

Hunter Maynard, like his father, was an intimidating sight, and she hoped fervently that their paths would not cross too often during her stay at Vogelsvlei.

She poured herself a cup of tea and drank it thirstily, but she had barely put down her cup when a step behind her made her glance over her shoulder to find Hunter Maynard observing her with a frowning intensity. Her nerves revolted at the sight of him, and everything within her suddenly cried out for escape, but the only exit was through the door which was filled by his bulk.

'I take it my mother is resting?' he questioned tersely, coming towards her and placing her at a distinct disadvantage which she lessened by pushing back her chair and rising quickly to her feet.

'That's correct, Mr Maynard.' Their glances clashed and, for some reason she could not explain, she felt herself driven to an apology. 'I know I'm not what you expected, but——'

'When I telephoned my aunt two weeks ago I made it absolutely clear to her that I required the services of an elderly nurse,' he interrupted in that same ferocious tone he had used to her from the start. 'I can't imagine what possessed her to send someone like you.'

He made her feel like an obnoxious insect which had crawled from beneath a stone to invade his home, and antagonism rose sharply within her. 'What exactly do you have against my being here, Mr Maynard?'

His brows drew together in an angry line above narrowed eyes. 'You're too young.'

'I'm twenty-four,' she replied, raising her chin defiantly, 'and I can assure you that I'm fully qualified, and quite capable of dealing with a case such as your mother's.'

'I don't doubt your capabilities, Sister Casey, but I still

say I would have preferred someone close to my mother's age.'

'Perhaps I should just mention one thing to you, Mr Maynard,' she retorted stiffly. 'There aren't many nurses these days who would agree to this sort of thing. Nurses taking on private patients are quite a thing of the past.'

'Why, then, did you accept?' he rapped out the question.

Her hazel eyes clouded and fell before the penetrating quality of his. 'I had my reasons.'

'Are you running away from a man,' he questioned cynically, 'or are you hoping to find one in this district?'

For the first time in her life Jennifer experienced the desire to strike a man, but she clenched her hands at her sides until her nails bit into her palms, and said with re- markable calmness, 'You're mistaken, Mr Maynard. My reasons for accepting this post have nothing to do with any living person.'

'Hasn't it?' His cynicism sliced right through her. 'I wonder . . .'

Anger surged through her like a flame licking at a raw wound and, raising her glance to his, she said icily, 'If you must have a reason for my being here, Mr Maynard, then it's because your aunt considered it would give me the opportunity to reconsider my resignation from the General Hospital in Cape Town.'

'According to my aunt, you've been at the General for some years,' he remarked coldly, 'or so Dr Tremayne led me to believe. I'm finding it rather difficult to accept that there's no man involved in this sudden decision of yours to resign.'

'Very well, there *was* a man involved . . . but he's dead,' she stated flatly, choking on the hurt she still found im- possible to erase. 'He died six months ago.'

'You've come here, then, to lick your wounds, so to speak?'

'If you want to think of it in that way, yes,' she replied, not at all surprised by his lack of compassion.

'This is not a rehabilitation centre, Sister Casey,' he informed her with a new harshness in his voice. 'You're here to take care of my mother, and that should keep you fully occupied.'

'I sincerely hope so,' she retorted swiftly and, sustaining his glowering glance, she added bitterly, 'You really do dislike the idea of having me here, don't you?'

'How very perceptive of you,' he replied with a hint of mockery in his voice. 'You're quite right, I dislike the idea of having you here in my house. I can only take the female of the species in small doses, and having one woman about the place has always been quite enough for me.'

'I shall make it my business to stay out of your way as much as possible, then,' she assured him, wondering vaguely at the stabbing discomfort she was experiencing.

'I sincerely hope you do,' he said tersely, moving his wide shoulders as if to ease the tension out of them. 'Isn't it about time you went to see if there's something you could do for my mother?'

Having this man remind her of her duties was almost a deliberate insult, but she swallowed down her anger and glanced at her watch before saying agreeably, 'So it is, Mr Maynard. If you'll excuse me.'

She wanted nothing more at that moment but to get away from this overbearing, disturbing, and aggravating man, but she had not quite reached the door when his harsh voice made her stop and turn to face him once more.

'Sister Casey,' he said, those blue eyes raking over her with a precision that set her nerves tingling with an uncomfortable awareness, 'please see to it that you keep your hair tied up like that at all times.'

Jennifer did not bother to answer him, but she felt murderous as she left the dining-room and marched down the passage towards Mrs Maynard's bedroom. If ever there was a man who had it in his power to bring out the worst in her, then it was Hunter Maynard! He was rude, arrogant, and totally without sensitivity. She disliked him intensely, and she had no doubt that the feeling was mutual. For some obscure, prejudiced reason, he did not want her there at Vogelsvlei, and if it were not for the simple reason that she did not want to disappoint Matron Griffiths, she would tell him exactly what she thought of him, and then he could do with his job just as he pleased for all she cared.

CHAPTER TWO

'I HOPE you're going to be happy here with us, Jennifer,' Alice Maynard expressed the wish that evening when Jennifer was helping her into bed and making her comfortable.

'Thank you, Mrs Maynard,' Jennifer smiled, straightening from her task.

'Don't go yet,' Mrs Maynard pleaded, her grey eyes smiling up at Jennifer. 'I'm not at all sleepy, and I'm so happy to be home that I feel as though I could quite happily lie awake for the pure pleasure of it.'

A warm, inner excitement was reflected in the eyes that met Jennifer's, and it was a look she had noticed on several occasions since their arrival on Vogelsvlei that afternoon.

'It's quite obvious to me that you love this farm very much.'

'Oh, yes,' the woman in her early sixties sighed contentedly. 'I've loved it from the moment I set foot on it, and I shall love it till the day I die.' There was unmistakable pride in her voice as she looked up suddenly and asked, 'Did you know that the Maynards have farmed here at Vogelsvlei for four generations?'

Jennifer shook her head. 'I'm afraid Matron Griffiths told me very little about your family history.'

'Sit down, my dear, and I'll tell you if you're interested.' She patted a space on the bed beside her and, when Jennifer was seated, she continued speaking. 'After my late husband's father died, my husband and his brother inherited

Vogelsvlei, but they found it impossible trying to farm together. My husband was a meticulous hard-working man,
while his brother was lazy and careless, and it was the latter
fact that drove my brother-in-law into an early grave. The
only solution to their problem, however, was to divide
Vogelsvlei into two, and to be quite fair they drew lots to
decide who would receive the portion of land with the
original homestead on it. My husband was fortunate in
that respect, and my late brother-in-law resignedly built
himself a home on the portion of land which is now called
Featherstone. Of course, since Hunter took over Vogelsvlei
he's bought several pieces of land adjoining ours, and the
farm is now almost twice the size it originally was.'

'And Featherstone?' Jennifer questioned curiously.

'Featherstone is exactly where it was all those years ago,'
Alice Maynard sighed. 'My nephew, Stanley, is very much
like his father, the poor, unfortunate soul. He's lazy, and
often careless, but I'm fond of the dear boy, and I can't
help feeling sorry for him.' A pained look flitted across her
remarkably smooth features. 'Hunter has tried to help him
in the past, to fire some enthusiasm into him, but Stanley
took exception to Hunter's assistance and has gone on just
as before.'

Alice Maynard's head went back against the pillows, and
the brightness of tears lurked in her eyes.

'I think you should try to go to sleep now, Mrs Maynard,'
Jennifer suggested, rising to her feet and straightening the
sheets where she had sat.

'Yes, I think I will.'

'Please don't hesitate to call me during the night if you
should need me.'

Alice Maynard gestured vaguely with her hand. 'I'll
manage.'

'No, you won't, Mrs Maynard,' Jennifer said at once when she saw those usually soft features set into a stubborn line. 'I must insist that you call me if you should require anything.'

A mischievous smile lurked in the grey eyes that met Jennifer's. 'Don't look so severe, child!'

'In my profession I sometimes have to be,' Jennifer warned, then an answering smile lifted the corners of her mouth. 'Goodnight, Mrs Maynard.'

'Goodnight, my dear,' Mrs Maynard echoed. 'I'll put off the light in a few moments.'

Jennifer nodded agreeably and left the room, but she almost collided with Hunter Maynard in the passage, and the sheer height and breadth of him was enough to make her nerve ends curl up into tight little knots.

'Is my mother asleep?' he queried in that harsh voice of his.

'Not yet, Mr Maynard,' she replied in her best Ward Sister's voice. 'You may go in, but don't keep her awake too long. She needs whatever rest she can get.'

'I'm well aware of that, Sister Casey,' he remarked cuttingly. 'You may go now.'

Dismissed, she turned away, and her low-heeled shoes made almost no sound on the carpeted floor as she walked into the hall and climbed the stairs up to her room. She had felt his eyes boring into her back until she had turned the corner towards the stairs, and for some unfathomable reason it disturbed her that this man should dislike her so much. She had come to Vogelsvlei to carry out her duties as a trained nurse, and when her task was completed she would leave. What harm was there in that? she wondered distractedly as she collected a few things in her room and crossed the passage towards the bathroom.

Jennifer tried to shut Hunter Maynard out of her thoughts, but she found it virtually impossible. He was not a man one could forget, not even after the briefest meeting, and the impact he had made on her that day had been something quite shattering. Within the space of a few hours she had discovered certain elements in her character which were quite shocking. Her calm confidence had very nearly disintegrated in the fiery furnace of an anger she had never dreamed herself capable of experiencing, and it was an anger which had driven her to the verge of a violence which she had imagined totally alien to her nature.

'Oh, *damm* the man!' she muttered eventually when she climbed into bed and switched off the light.

Her first night at Vogelsvlei was a restless one, and she could not blame it entirely on the strangeness of her surroundings, and neither could she blame Alice Maynard, who had called her only once during the night. It was Hunter's intensely blue and ferocious eyes which haunted her persistently through the night until she had grave doubts about her decision to accept this post in the Maynard home. It was too late now to turn back, and going forward was the only way out of this situation which she had so innocently landed herself in.

Jennifer awoke to a curious booming sound echoing across the silent veld the following morning, and it was only after questioning Mrs Maynard that she discovered it was the sound made by the male ostrich when courting his female, or when challenging an interfering male in the adjoining camp. This information made Jennifer intensely curious to know more about these strange birds, but it would have to wait until she had a free moment to explore the farm, she decided regretfully.

The breakfast-room was spacious and sunny, and Jennifer

could not help but admire the beautifully preserved yellowwood table with the stinkwood base. She ran the tips of her slender fingers lightly and appreciatively over the polished surface, but when she happened to look up she found Hunter observing her intently from beneath frowning dark brows.

'You have some magnificent pieces of furniture in your home,' she commented with selfconscious sincerity as she lowered her trembling hand on to her lap beneath the table. Why she should feel guilty at being caught admiring one of the Maynard family's possessions, she had no idea, and Hunter's reply did not exactly make her feel any better.

'They are all selective and expensive items gathered over the years,' he said with a suggestion of derisive mockery in his voice.

'My late husband's father had several pieces imported from Europe during those years when the market price for ostrich feathers rocketed so high,' Alice Maynard explained, her warm, unpretentious manner making Jennifer feel slightly more at ease. 'This table, however, was bought almost forty years ago when my husband and I went down to Knysna on our honeymoon.'

'One would never think this table is as old as that,' Jennifer remarked in surprise.

'That's because my mother looks after each item of furniture as if it were her most treasured possession,' Hunter explained, and again there was that hint of mockery in his voice.

'I happen to love wood, and I mean any kind of wood,' Alice Maynard stated almost defensively.

'I know, Mother.' One large hand reached out across the table to clasp Alice's in a surprisingly gentle manner. 'It's a pity not everyone shares your passion for the items nature has provided us with.'

He smiled at his mother, and it was a smile that did something extraordinary to Jennifer's insides. The cold, glittering hardness in his eyes was replaced by a tender warmth, and the harshly chiselled mouth assumed a more humane appearance. The transformation was brief but incredible, and Jennifer hated to think what would happen to her one day should Hunter Maynard deign to smile at her in that way.

She brushed aside this disturbing thought with some urgency, and concentrated instead on her breakfast of ostrich egg which had been scrambled and richly spiced, but she could not deny that she was becoming increasingly conscious of the man seated at the head of the table. He looked tough and incredibly masculine in khaki pants and short-sleeved bush jacket, and beneath her lowered lashes she observed the fine dark hair on his muscled forearms, which were as deeply tanned as his rugged features. She was convinced that he was as strong as an ox, judging by the width of his shoulders and the size of his hands, and she dreaded to think of what might happen if he were ever driven to violence. She shuddered inwardly at this frightening image flashing across her mind, and poured their coffee at Alice Maynard's request. Hunter declined, however, and left the breakfast-room to go out and inspect the new fencing he was having erected somewhere on the farm.

From her wheelchair, Alice Maynard issued instructions to the servants and checked the supplies, but she was not content for long with being confined to the house, and Jennifer watched over her carefully as she wheeled herself out on to the verandah to survey the garden and the fields beyond it. It was a warm morning, and Jennifer could not object to Mrs Maynard's desire to spend it out on the spacious verandah with its trellised railings and carved wooden pillars which had been painted a cool white. Bright yellow daffodils and crimson roses provided a vivid splash of colour at the bottom end of the sunlit garden, and Jennifer breathed deeply on the fresh country air. The peaceful silence was disturbed only by the birdsong in the trees, and the occasional booming which emerged from a male ostrich to reverberate across the veld, and, as Jennifer lowered herself into a cane chair, she could not help but envy Alice Maynard for being able to call this peaceful haven her home.

Hunter arrived just as tea was brought out on to the verandah, and the cane chair creaked protestingly beneath his weight when he seated himself a little distance from Jennifer. She poured their tea, and listened absently to the conversation he was having with his mother, but their voices ceased abruptly some minutes later when a red sports car zoomed up the drive and came to a gravel-crunching halt close to the verandah.

A young girl, with long black hair and a trim, curvaceous figure leapt from the car and tripped buoyantly up the steps towards them. She was young, probably twenty, Jennifer decided as her admiring glance lingered on the liquid-brown eyes, and the sensuously curved crimson mouth which had parted in a flashing smile which was directed solely at Hunter, who sat observing her with a faintly humorous smile curving his mouth.

'I'm just in time for tea, it seems,' her lilting voice exclaimed as she pulled up a chair and seated herself beside Hunter, and only then did her glance shift towards Alice Maynard. 'It's so nice to see you home again, Mrs Maynard,' she remarked sweetly, but Jennifer sensed a hint of insincerity in her voice, and wondered why.

'Thank you, Carla,' Alice Maynard replied and, gesturing towards the silent girl in the white, clinical overall who was seated close beside her, she said: 'May I introduce Sister Jennifer Casey? Jennifer, this is Carla von Brandis. Her father farms not far from here.'

The two girls acknowledged each other politely, but Jennifer had a peculiar feeling that she was being critically examined for some reason she had yet to discover.

'Forgive me if I'm wrong,' Carla said, accepting a cup of tea from Jennifer, and directing her liquid gaze at Hunter, 'but I was under the impression that you were acquiring the services of an older nurse.'

His mouth twisted cynically, and that hard blue gaze sliced through Jennifer as he said: 'I was under that same impression, but my dear aunt in Cape Town obviously decided differently.'

'And I'm very glad she did,' Alice Maynard interjected sharply.

During the brief silence which followed Alice's statement Jennifer sensed a certain animosity between her patient and this young girl with the flowing dark hair and the flashing eyes beneath sweeping dark brows. It puzzled her, but she did not dwell on it when Carla turned to her with an engaging smile on her lips.

'Forgive me, Sister Casey, I didn't intend my remark to sound rude.'

'I was not offended, Miss von Brandis,' Jennifer replied with her usual calm, but she could not resist darting a glance in Hunter's direction as she added: 'I'm well aware of the fact that I'm not at all what Mr Maynard had hoped I'd be.'

Carla was quick to notice the hostile glance Hunter shot in Jennifer's direction, and she grasped the situation with remarkable swiftness.

'Darling, have you been boorish to Sister Casey?' she demanded of Hunter in that lilting, humorous voice which she seemed to reserve for him alone.

'Drink your tea,' he answered abruptly, rising to his feet to tower over them all. 'I have something to show you.'

Carla pouted prettily. 'You're a bully, Hunter, and I don't know why I put up with you.'

'Are you coming or aren't you?' he demanded curtly, turning towards the steps leading off the verandah.

'I'm coming,' Carla replied, hastily swallowing down the remainder of her tea and getting to her feet. 'See you later,' she flung the words over her shoulder and, with her hands clinging to Hunter's arm, they disappeared round the side of the house.

'She's beautiful,' Jennifer could not help remarking towards Mrs Maynard.

'And spoilt,' Alice Maynard added tersely. 'I've known her since she was a child of six, and I can't say that I've ever really taken a fancy to her.'

'Your son seems to be fond of her,' Jennifer said, recalling the look in his eyes when Carla had arrived.

'She's the only girl he's been able to tolerate since——' Alice stopped abruptly, shaking her grey head and gesturing distastefully. 'Pour me another cup of tea, dear, and let's talk about pleasanter things.'

Jennifer did as she was told, but she was left to wonder what, exactly, Alice Maynard had been about to say. Carla von Brandis was the only girl Hunter had been able to tolerate since—since what? Various possibilities came to mind, but Jennifer decided finally that it would be safer not to speculate about something which was absolutely no concern of hers.

Carla returned to the house with Hunter and stayed to lunch, but she left shortly after Jennifer had taken Mrs Maynard to her room and, affected by the country air, Jennifer went up to her own room to rest for a while.

Later that afternoon two more visitors arrived at Vogelsvlei, and Jennifer was introduced to Kate Maynard and her son Stanley. Kate was a thin, gaunt-looking woman, but she had a friendly face and a ready smile. Her son Stanley was tall, lean, and dark, with hungry-looking grey eyes, and they seemed to seek out Jennifer at every turn. She was, at first, not sure whether to feel flattered or embarrassed, but she finally settled for ignoring him as much as possible.

Agnes served tea and cream scones on the wide, cool verandah, and, when Alice and Kate became involved in a family discussion, Jennifer found that she could no longer ignore Stanley.

'Tell me, Jennifer,' he began with an easy familiarity as he pulled his chair closer to hers, 'have you ever been on an ostrich farm before?'

'No, never.'

His hungry glance swept over her once more. 'I don't suppose you've had time as yet to take a look around?'

'No, I haven't, I'm afraid,' she replied, shaking her head.

'You should ask Hunter to show you around,' he suggested with a hint of sarcasm in his voice which startled her. 'There isn't a thing about ostrich farming he couldn't tell you.'

'I wouldn't dream of encroaching on Mr Maynard's time in that way, and besides . . .' She glanced quickly at the man in question, but his attention was fortunately elsewhere, and she added in a lowered voice, 'I'm kept much too busy.'

'Surely you have a little time to yourself during the day?' Stanley demanded, the indignant expression on his face bringing a smile to her lips.

'You forget, perhaps, Mr Maynard, that I only arrived here yesterday.'

'Yes, of course,' he acknowledged, 'and I'd be honoured if you would call me Stanley. You can reserve the "Mr Maynard" for Hunter, if you wish.'

She looked up suddenly to find Hunter's hostile blue gaze resting on her and, for some inexplicable reason, she smiled at the man beside her with considerably more warmth than she had originally intended. 'Thank you . . . Stanley.'

Encouraged, Stanley said: 'I hope you'll accept my invitation to come out to Featherstone with me some day soon?'

Jennifer hesitated, but only briefly. 'I'd like that very much.'

Stanley Maynard was really quite harmless, she decided afterwards, but throughout the remainder of their conversation she was given the distinct impression that there was a great deal of animosity between the two cousins, and she could not quite make up her mind who or what was to blame for it. It could, of course, be jealousy, but she did not like to dwell on the thought.

At dinner that evening Jennifer discovered that Nellie had prepared marinated ostrich steak with mushroom sauce and fresh young vegetables.

'It's Nellie's speciality,' Alice Maynard explained, cutting into her steak with an enthusiasm Jennifer could not quite match at that moment.

She eyed the steak on her plate rather dubiously, but when

she glimpsed the mocking expression in Hunter's eyes as he observed her she thrust aside her doubts and tasted it.

The steak was tender, succulent, and slightly sweet, and when she looked up eventually to find two pairs of eyes observing her, she smiled selfconsciously and murmured appreciatively, 'It's delicious.'

A smile of satisfaction lit up Alice Maynard's face, but Hunter did not quite lose his mocking expression as Jennifer went on to enjoy her dinner.

Later that evening, when Jennifer left Mrs Maynard's room to go up to her own, she encountered Hunter in the hall, but instead of allowing her to go on up the stairs, he barred her way.

'You found my cousin entertaining?' he asked cynically.

'He was friendly and polite,' she replied awkwardly, and she could have added, 'Which is more than I can say for you,' but she decided against it.

'Stanley is friendly and polite to anything that happens to wear a skirt,' Hunter remarked derisively. 'I should warn you, though, he's unreliable, and not much of a financial catch.'

Jennifer stiffened at once, and a coldness seeped into her voice. 'Thanks for the warning, but it's quite unnecessary.'

'Do you think so?' he mocked her.

'I don't merely think so, I know it.'

'You're hoping to land a bigger fish, then?'

His cynicism and his mockery once more stirred up the flame of her anger, but she suppressed it with the greatest difficulty to ask, 'What makes you so sure, Mr Maynard, that I'm out to get myself a man?'

'Catching some poor sap, and dangling him on a line is woman's whole existence,' he told her derisively.

'You have a poor opinion of women in general, Mr Maynard,' she informed him, bristling with fury, 'or is that solely your opinion of me?'

'Women are all the same,' he replied harshly, his disparaging glance raking over her until her body grew taut with dislike. 'They think that once they have their claws hooked into a man they can do with him as they please.'

'Has Miss von Brandis led you to the stage where she can do with you as she pleases?'

There was an explosive silence that left her wondering if she had not gone too far, then he said coldly, 'Kindly leave Carla out of this discussion, Sister Casey.'

Subdued, but not defeated, Jennifer said: 'Am I to understand that your distorted opinion of women doesn't include Miss von Brandis?'

'Carla is a very special girl,' he replied, his eyes hooded.

'So it seems.'

A cynical smile played about that harsh mouth of his. 'Do I detect a note of sarcasm in your voice, Sister Casey?'

'It was not my intention to be sarcastic, Mr Maynard,' she assured him coldly. 'Now, if you'll excuse me, I'd like to go up to my room.'

It looked for a moment as if he were going to ignore her request, then he stood aside, and she mounted the stairs as quickly as she could, but she could feel his eyes boring into her back until she was out of his sight.

He was an impossible man, she decided when she reached the seclusion of her room. She had sworn to stay out of his way as much as possible, but she realised now that it was virtually impossible to avoid someone while living under the same roof with them, and heaven only knew how she was going to tolerate Hunter Maynard during the weeks to follow.

'For goodness' sake, child!' Alice Maynard exclaimed one morning when Jennifer had settled her comfortably on the verandah. 'I shall be perfectly all right here with my crocheting, and there must be something you'd rather do than to sit here with me.'

Jennifer looked a little dubious at first, but then she smiled and nodded. 'I always enjoy keeping you company, but perhaps I'll go for a short stroll.'

'That's a good idea,' Alice agreed goodnaturedly. 'It will be quite some time before Agnes brings our tea.'

After making sure that her patient had everything she required, Jennifer took a walk down to the camps nearest to the house, and it was there that she met Danny. He was inspecting the bales of dry lucerne which had been dropped off in the camps, and when he saw Jennifer approaching he respectfully raised his wide-brimmed felt hat.

'*Dag, nonnie*,' he smiled, and Jennifer's own lips curved into a smile as she walked up to him.

'Good morning, Danny,' she returned his greeting.

There was a barrier of awkwardness between them as she allowed her glance to stray out across the camps, taking in the quaint inverted V's of the thatched nesting shelters which had been erected for the ostriches, but her curiosity finally broke through Danny's barrier of restraint, and she found him an informative and amusing companion. His English was punctuated with Afrikaans words, and so it came as no surprise to her that he should refer to the male ostrich as a *mannetjie*, and the female as a *wyfie*.

'Why are there only two ostriches in this camp, Danny?' she asked curiously, her eyes lingering on the large birds grazing near the fence.

'They want to breed, *nonnie*, and then the *mannetjie* is very *kwaai*,' he explained. 'With that sharp nail on his big toe he can kill another *mannetjie*, or he could be killed himself.'

Jennifer eyed the man beside her with a certain amount of disbelief. 'Are they really that vicious?'

'*Nonnie?*' he shook his head and whistled through his teeth. 'I've seen a *mannetjie* kick a big man like myself and tear his chest open from the throat down.' He pointed to the male bird with its black body feathers and white wing plumes. 'When a *mannetjie*'s beak and the front of his legs are red like this one's, then you must stay away from him, *nonnie*, because it's a sure sign that he's broody, and then he's dangerous.'

The male bird uttered that booming sound she had heard before as it followed the drab-coloured female across to the far side of the camp, and his graceful neck was raised proudly now as he flapped his wings and tripped lightly after her.

'How much would you say an ostrich weighs?' she questioned Danny, anxious to know more.

'A *mannetjie* like this one could weigh almost three times your weight, *nonnie*,' he told her, then his attention was diverted towards one of the nearby camps, and he swore lightly under his breath. 'Excuse me, *nonnie*. That stupid Pieta has left that gate open, and the chicks are going to come out.'

There was no time for Jennifer to reply, for Danny was already dashing across towards the camp where the inquisitive chicks were rapidly approaching the gate which had been left open accidentally.

'Hey, Pieta!' she heard Danny shouting angrily. '*My magtig, man!* What do you think you're doing?'

At the sound of Danny's angry voice, Pieta, a young boy, jumped off the trailer behind the stationary tractor and, realising his error, he ran towards the gate and closed it with seconds to spare as the chicks were preparing themselves for a bold dash out of the camp.

Jennifer's attention wandered back, however, towards the two fully grown ostriches just beyond the fence where she was standing. The hen, with her head lowered and her wings outstretched, seemed to be enticing the male, and he responded at once by going down on to his knees. With his wings outstretched to form a straight line across his breast, he lowered his neck until his head was on a level with his back, then he swung his head and neck from side to side rhythmically as he courted his mate. The hen, unpredictable like most females perhaps, suddenly displayed a total lack of interest, and wandered further away from the male, who finally relinquished his amorous efforts to capture his lady's attention.

A strong breeze came up across the sun-drenched veld as Jennifer continued her observation of the ostriches. It stirred the leaves of the pepper trees and, before she could prevent it, it lifted the brightly coloured scarf from about her neck and swept it over the fence into the camp.

If it had been any other scarf, Jennifer would not have bothered with retrieving it, but it was one of the last things Colin had given her before his death, and she could not leave it there to be trampled, eaten, or torn to shreds.

The ostriches were both on the far side of the camp and, calculating the distance from the gate to where her scarf lay, she decided she could quite easily retrieve it and reach the gate before either of the ostriches were any the wiser. She lifted the chain off the gate-post and stepped into the camp, but the male ostrich had been quick to notice the colourful object lying in the veld, and he had raised his head warily to observe it with a natural inquisitiveness before approaching it. It was too late now to change her mind, and she could still make it if she was quick about it, she decided firmly.

'*Nonnie!*' she heard Danny shouting to her from a distance. 'Nonnie Jennifer! Get out of there quickly!'

She *had* to get her scarf back, she told herself and, turning a deliberately deaf ear to Danny's instructions, she dashed into the camp and sprinted across to where her scarf lay caught up in the grass. The male bird could not avoid seeing her now, and he approached threateningly, his wings flapping and a hissing sound emerging from his parted beak. His speed was incredible, she realised as, paralysed with fear, she stood there facing the charging bird, her scarf clutched in her damp hands, and her heart beating in her throat.

'*Run, nonnie, run!*' Danny shouted, and the sound of his raised voice somehow activated her limbs.

Taking one last look at the infuriated bird, she ran as if the devil himself was treading on her heels. She could not quite remember afterwards what exactly had happened, but Danny was there in the camp with her, and he was shouting something to her while waving a long thorn tree branch at the hissing ostrich.

'Get behind me, *nonnie!*' his instruction finally penetrated her numbed brain. '*Get behind me!*'

There was a soaring in her ears, and for one dreadful moment she thought she was going to faint, but she did as she was told and, miraculously, he held the ostrich at bay with that thorny branch while he backed her and himself towards safety.

She knew, without doubt, that she had faced death a few moments ago because of her thoughtless action, but she faced another kind of death when a large hand gripped her arm and jerked her roughly aside.

'Make sure that gate is shut, Danny!' Hunter Maynard thundered, and without waiting to see whether Danny carried out his instruction, he steered Jennifer unceremoniously towards the ancient pepper tree some distance away. It was only when they stood beneath its welcome shade that he jerked her to a halt and swung her round so that she was left with no option but to look up into eyes which were flashing blue flames of fury. 'What the devil did you think you were doing?' he demanded in a voice that made her quake inwardly.

'I'm sorry, but I——' She swallowed convulsively. 'I can explain.'

'I'm waiting!' he savagely rapped out the words.

Shaking from head to foot, and with a mouth as dry as the dust beneath her feet, she said: 'My scarf blew into the camp. The ostriches were grazing on the far side, and I thought it would be quite safe to slip in quickly to retrieve it.'

Her explanation, put into words, seemed foolish now, and Hunter obviously thought so too, for his contemptuous glance raked her mercilessly. 'So you thought you could outpace an ostrich that can manage anything up to thirty miles an hour?'

'I—I never thought anything of the kind. I——' His blazing glance conquered her angry defiance and, lowering her eyes before his, she murmured helplessly, 'I'm sorry.'

'What was so important about that scarf anyway?' he demanded harshly, ignoring her apology.

'It—It was a gift.'

'My God, I could strangle you!' he announced gratingly, taking both her arms in a tight grip and shaking her forcefully while he glowered at her. 'Do you realise that your stupid sentimentality nearly cost you your life?'

'You're h-hurting me,' she managed with difficulty, biting down hard on her lip to prevent herself from crying out, and he released her at once with a force that sent her staggering back against the rough stem of the tree.

'Get yourself back to the house,' he ordered harshly, the muscles in his jaw standing out prominently as if in an effort to control his anger. 'And if you want to behave like an irresponsible child, then I suggest you stay away from these camps in future.'

Feeling utterly foolish, but clinging desperately to the remnants of her dignity and shattered composure, she walked back to the house with the withering sensation that those blazing, contemptuous eyes were following her every uncomfortable step of the way.

CHAPTER THREE

JENNIFER'S hair had come undone during her disturbing ordeal at the hands of Hunter Maynard, her white overall clung limply to her damp body, and there was a dirty smudge across her one hot cheek where she had wiped away a stray tear, but it was nothing compared to the way she had been shaken inwardly.

Alice Maynard took one look at her when she stepped on to the verandah before she exclaimed with concern, 'For goodness' sake, child! What happened to you?'

'My scarf blew into one of the camps,' Jennifer explained briefly.

'Don't tell me,' Alice remarked, looking quite horrified. 'You went in to fetch it, and the ostrich charged you.'

Jennifer sat down heavily on the cane chair and nodded miserably. 'Yes, I'm afraid so.'

'My dear, how could you have done such a ridiculous thing!'

'I couldn't leave the scarf at the mercy of the ostriches,' she confided unhappily. 'It's one of the last things Colin gave me before he died.'

'Colin?'

'Dr Colin Ashton,' Jennifer replied, looking up into those curiously intent grey eyes. 'We were engaged to be married.'

'I understand,' Alice Maynard nodded, her glance sympathetic now, 'but don't risk your life in that way again.'

Jennifer shuddered and pulled the remaining pins from

her hair before shaking it free, and her action trapped the sunlight in it to accentuate its golden sheen. 'It was foolish of me, I know, and it won't happen again.'

Alice Maynard nodded, then a frown settled between her brows. 'You'd better not let Hunter hear of this.'

'I'm afraid he knows already,' Jennifer confided, grimacing as she examined the bruises on her arms where his hands had bitten into the soft flesh. 'He arrived just as Danny was edging me out of the gate.'

'Oh, dear!' Alice sighed, clasping her hands together in prayer-like fashion. 'I suppose he was furious?'

'I was more than furious, Mother. I was murderous!' a deep, thundering voice replied, and both women swung round in their chairs to face the man coming up behind them. 'When I think of what might have happened, I could shake her all over again,' he added menacingly.

'Hunter, you didn't!' his mother exclaimed reprovingly.

'Be thankful that I didn't thrash her!' he rasped explosively, his eyes burning down into Jennifer's before taking in the disarray of her silky hair.

'Hunter!' his mother repeated in that reproving voice, but Jennifer rose from her chair to face him before Alice Maynard could continue speaking.

'I'm well aware of my stupidity in going into that camp, Mr Maynard, and I promise you, it won't happen again.'

'I should hope not!' he barked at her, making her flinch inwardly. 'What on earth possessed you to risk your life for a silly piece of silk?' he demanded, making a disparaging gesture towards the scarf she still clutched in her hand.

'It was a gift from her late fiancé,' Alice Maynard replied before Jennifer could stop her.

There was an incredulous silence, then a look of black fury flashed across his hard, angular features as he said bitingly, 'Well, she very nearly joined him in whatever realm he's progressed to.'

Jennifer winced inwardly and paled. 'I think I'll go upstairs and tidy up before tea, if you don't mind.'

Hunter's hard glance never gave her a moment's peace for the rest of the day. Whenever they met he would look at her as if he wished he could burn holes right through her, and no matter how much she tried to avoid him, he was always there, his large frame barring her way, or close within range as if he were observing her every move.

She felt relieved that night when she could at last return to the privacy of her room, but she felt restless after her bath and, tightening the belt of her silk robe about her waist, she pushed open the glass doors leading out on to the balcony and stepped outside.

It was a warm, scented night, with the sky studded with stars, and as she looked out across the darkened veld towards the Swartberg mountains, a tired little sigh escaped her. After almost two weeks at Vogelsvlei, she no longer found the silence strange, and if it were not for Hunter Maynard's hateful attitude, she could almost say she was happy and contented in her new surroundings.

'It's a perfect night, isn't it?' a deep voice remarked behind her, and her body tensed as she turned to face the dark shape leaning against the wall a little distance from her. How long had he been standing there? she wondered frantically, and what must he think of her wandering about in her robe and slippered feet?

'Have you suddenly lost your tongue, Sister Casey?' he mocked her, looking infinitely dangerous in his black slacks and matching shirt, and she backed involuntarily against the railing as he approached her.

'I'm surprised you should speak to me in this civilised

manner, Mr Maynard,' she said the first thing that came to mind, a strange fluttering in her breast when he stepped into the patch of light coming from her bedroom.

'I'm always civilised, except when crossed,' he replied mockingly, and she almost jumped out of her skin when his fingers brushed lightly against her arm below the short sleeve of her robe. 'Did I do this?' he asked softly.

She lowered her glance to where his fingers explored the bluish marks beneath her skin, and it was with some difficulty that she said: 'I bruise easily.'

'I shall have to remember that.'

His voice sounded odd, but it was nothing compared to the odd feelings his light, almost caressing touch was arousing within her. Her pulse leapt wildly and, stepping away from him, she said jerkily, 'Goodnight, Mr Maynard.'

'Dr Tremayne telephoned,' his voice stopped her before she could enter her room. 'He's coming out to Vogelsvlei tomorrow morning to see my mother.'

She turned to glance back at him, and experienced again that violent reaction to his physical appearance which reminded her of their first meeting in the hospital. She was conscious, too, of his disapproving glance on her hair as it hung loosely about her shoulders, and she said tritely, 'Thank you for telling me.'

'Goodnight, Sister Casey,' he said abruptly now, and he was gone before she could reply.

Jennifer was frowning when she stepped into her room and closed the doors firmly behind her. Hunter Maynard was a disturbing and often puzzling man. Those hands which had inflicted pain that very morning had moments ago caressed the bruises left by his brutal fingers, and it had been a devastating experience. That light touch had awakened dormant nerves, and it had quickened unheard-of pulses, but most of all it had made her aware of how susceptible she was to a gentle word, or touch, from this man who had declared himself her enemy from the moment they had met. She did not want to delve too deeply into her feelings, but what she suspected was enough to shake the foundations of her existence, and it was perhaps best that she did not dwell on the subject.

Jennifer heard Dr Tremayne's car coming up the drive towards the house shortly after eight the following morning and, leaving Alice Maynard fully dressed and resting on her bed, she walked out on to the verandah to find Hunter already there.

'It seems as though Dr Tremayne has brought someone with him this time,' he remarked frowningly.

Jennifer's glance followed the direction of his, and she caught her breath in surprise when she saw the tall, lean man in his early thirties climbing out of the car and accompanying Dr Tremayne towards the house.

Mike Hoffman had changed very little over the years, she decided with a touch of humour. He was wearing his dark hair considerably shorter, but the lean, tanned face was still as handsome as ever. He looked up suddenly, and a look of surprise flashed across his face as his eyes met hers.

'Jennifer!' he exclaimed, his white teeth flashing in a familiar smile as he leapt up the steps and kissed her quite deliberately on the lips.

Aware of the two men who had witnessed that little scene, Jennifer blushed scarlet, and murmured self-consciously, 'Hello, Mike.'

'Well, for heaven's sake!' he laughed down at her. 'I never imagined I would ever meet you again, and most certainly not here on a farm in Oudtshoorn.'

'You two know each other?' Hunter asked unnecessarily, his tight-lipped expression filling her with a sense of fore-boding.

'Jennifer and I have known each other since she was a student nurse and I a fledgling doctor,' Mike announced, draping his arm comfortably about Jennifer's shoulders as he glanced down at her for confirmation. 'Isn't that so, darling?'

Mike's 'darling' meant nothing, but Hunter, whose eyes had narrowed at the sound of it, that word obviously spoke volumes, and, rising to the occasion, she glanced up at Mike and smiled a little provocatively as she said: 'Don't divulge all our secrets, Mike.'

'Well, I must say it's good to see you again after all this time,' he remarked, hugging her against him before he released her.

'Perhaps you would like to come inside,' Hunter said stonily. 'My mother is expecting you.'

Dr Tremayne, who had not spoken a word since their arrival, gestured to Mike to follow him, and somehow Jennifer ended up at the rear with Hunter's eyes boring into her back once more until her skin crawled. Fortunately he did not follow them into his mother's bedroom, and the incredible tension within her eased considerably while Dr Tremayne and Mike examined Alice Maynard with a thoroughness which almost succeeded in tiring her out.

The instructions Jennifer received were explicit. Her patient was to be allowed more freedom of movement, the daily exercises were to continue, and Dr Tremayne agreed with Mike that Mrs Maynard could try walking with crutches. It was arranged over tea that Hunter would pick them up at the hospital the following day, and with Mrs Maynard firmly ensconced on the verandah with Dr

Tremayne and Hunter for company, Mike drew Jennifer aside and out into the garden where they could talk privately.

'How long have you been looking after Mrs Maynard, Jennifer?' he asked when they were some distance away from the house.

'It will be two weeks this coming Monday,' she replied, aware of Hunter's brooding glance following their progress across the lawn. She could well imagine what was going on in his twisted mind, but being with an old and trusted friend like Mike Hoffman was enough to obliterate her cares.

'I imagined you'd be safely married to Colin by now,' he interrupted her thoughts. 'What happened to change your mind?'

Of all things, she had never imagined that Mike had not heard of Colin's death, and, taking the task upon herself, she said quietly, 'Colin died almost seven months ago.'

Mike's dark eyes looked bleak as they met hers. 'I'm sorry, Jennifer.'

'I thought you knew.'

'No one passed the news on to me, and I'm afraid I don't get much time to read the newspapers these days.' He took her arm and guided her towards the shade of the pepper trees. 'Tell me what happened.'

Jennifer sighed as she picked a leaf off the tree and twisted it between her fingers. 'You must remember how crazy he used to be about flying.'

'I remember,' Mike smiled reminiscently. 'He used to spend every free moment careering about the sky.' His hand tightened on Jennifer's arm. 'He crashed his Cessna, is that it?'

'He overshot the runway for some reason, and ploughed

into the trees,' she explained, the horror of it all swimming before her eyes. 'The fuel tank exploded almost at once.'

'Were you there when it happened?'

'Yes, I was there,' she nodded, then she shut her mind to the memory of that terrifying morning on the airfield, and said firmly, 'Let's talk about something else.'

'I second that.'

She glanced up at Mike curiously. 'Are you married yet?'

'Not a chance,' he laughed, his eyes crinkling up at the corners in the old familiar way. 'I intend playing the field for some time before I put the noose of marriage around my neck.'

Her smile was slightly admonishing, but when she glanced back at the house, she said: 'It looks as though Dr Tremayne is ready to leave.'

'I hope we'll meet again, Jennifer, and I don't mean under these circumstances,' he remarked as they strolled back towards the house. 'Will you have dinner with me some time?'

'I'm afraid I can't promise you anything,' she replied ruefully. 'I must be here if Mrs Maynard should need me. You understand that, don't you?'

'You'll find my telephone number in the book,' he persisted. 'Give me a ring if you have any free time, and I'll think up something entertaining.'

'I can imagine what that "something entertaining" will be,' she laughed knowingly, and an injured look flashed across his lean face.

'I've always been on my best behaviour with you, haven't I?'

'Only because I've always been able to see right through you,' she reminded him humorously.

'That's unfortunately true,' he grinned down at her moments before they joined the others.

Jennifer had a few words with Dr Tremayne and Mike when they eventually walked out to the car, but she was conscious of Hunter's glowering expression as he accompanied them, and it made her feel decidedly uncomfortable.

'See you, darling,' Mike said lightly, winking at Jennifer as he climbed into Dr Tremayne's car, and when it disappeared down the drive Hunter turned to face Jennifer with that familiar chilling hostility in his glance.

'Knowing Mike Hoffman's reputation with women, I take it that you and he were lovers once?'

Jennifer's first reaction was one of anger, then she changed her mind and said lightly, 'You may take it whichever way you please.'

'Quite a coincidence, isn't it, that you should run into each other here in Oudtshoorn—and very convenient too, I might add,' Hunter remarked, narrowing his mocking eyes against the sun, and Jennifer clenched her right hand at her side when she felt her palm itching with the desire to make violent contact with his smug face.

'Your insinuations that I knew of Mike's presence here in Oudtshoorn are quite unfounded, but it *is* convenient meeting an old friend once again,' she replied, and she would have walked up to the house to join Alice Maynard on the verandah if steely fingers had not latched on to her wrist.

'What you do in your free time is no concern of mine, Sister Casey, but I hope you don't intend to neglect my mother.'

She twisted her wrist free of his disturbing touch and raised her glance to find his eyes blazing down into hers with a contemptuous look that seemed to sear her soul, and she resorted to defiance as her only weapon against the inexplicable pain lunging through her heart.

'I'm not in the habit of neglecting my duties, Mr Maynard,' she said, raising her chin and holding his glance, 'and personal pleasures have always had to take second place.'

His mouth tightened ominously. 'I'm very glad to hear that.'

Hunter strode off in the opposite direction to what Jennifer was taking and, thankful for this slight respite, she joined Alice Maynard on the verandah.

'I have been hoping that your relationship with my son would improve in time, but it seems as though my hopes were in vain,' Mrs Maynard observed shrewdly, her glance travelling to the imprint of Hunter's fingers which were still clearly visible against Jennifer's wrist.

'Don't let it trouble you, Mrs Maynard.'

Alice's grey glance rested on the white-clad figure of the slim young woman seated in the cane chair opposite her, then a slight frown appeared on her brow. 'How well do you know Dr Hoffman?'

The question was unexpected, but Jennifer's calm expression did not waver for an instant. 'I've known him since I was a student nurse, but he left Cape Town eighteen months ago, and somehow we lost contact with each other, as neither of us are very good correspondents.'

'Was he someone special?'

'Not in the way you mean, Mrs Maynard,' Jennifer replied with a spark of laughter in her hazel eyes. 'He was a special friend, and nothing more.'

The older woman lowered her glance a little guiltily. 'I suppose you think I'm a prying old woman.'

It was a statement, not a question, and Jennifer's glance softened as she leaned forward in her chair to clasp her patient's hands. 'I think you're a wonderfully warm-hearted person who takes an avid interest in the people around her, and that's a quality I admire very much.'

The conversation drifted in a different direction after that, and mainly to Dr Tremayne's suggestion that Alice Maynard was improving to the extent that she could make use of crutches in future, instead of relying so constantly on the wheelchair. She was excited about this development, and confessed that she could hardly wait for Hunter to collect the crutches in town that afternoon.

Jennifer did not see Hunter again until they sat down to lunch, and then he ignored Jennifer completely by speaking only to his mother. It hurt, strangely enough, but she was determined not to let his manner affect her in any serious way.

'I'm going to my room,' Alice Maynard said at last, and Jennifer rose thankfully from the table to accompany her from the dining-room.

Hunter was nowhere in sight when Jennifer stepped out on to the verandah some minutes later to see Stanley Maynard climb out of his car and walk towards her where she awaited him on the steps.

'Good afternoon, Stanley,' she welcomed him with a smile and, feeling a little uncomfortable under that hungry glance of his, she said quickly, 'I'm sorry, but Mrs Maynard is resting at the moment. She would have been glad to see you, though.'

'I came to see you, Jennifer.'

'Oh,' she managed, taken aback.

'I'm on my way to town, and I thought you might like to go in with me,' he explained, his imploring glance meeting hers.

'I'm afraid I can't come with you.'

Anger instantly sparked in his eyes. 'Aunt Alice certainly keeps you securely tied to her wheelchair, doesn't she?'

'It's not like that, Stanley, and you know it,' she replied gently. 'Until your aunt is more mobile I must stay close in case I'm needed.'

'Yes, of course, I know that,' he acknowledged grudgingly. 'Is there anything I could get you in town?' he asked after a moment of deliberation.

'You could perhaps save Mr Maynard a trip into town by collecting his mother's crutches from the hospital.'

'Not on your life, I won't!' he brushed aside her suggestion roughly, and Jennifer glanced at him in surprise.

'Why don't you like your cousin?'

'I can't stand smart alecks who always think they know better than anyone else,' he replied with a sullen look on his face as she walked with him towards his car. 'Hunter thought once he could come and shunt me around on my own farm, but he was mistaken,' he added fiercely.

Jennifer could think of nothing to say, not after having heard from Alice Maynard how Hunter had tried to give assistance to his cousin who was by nature a lazy, unmethodical farmer, and she could not help thinking again that Stanley's angry remarks had been sparked off by a certain amount of jealousy and envy.

'Jennifer . . .' Stanley's hands gripped hers unexpectedly. 'You will come out to Featherstone with me one day soon, won't you?'

Jennifer had always felt a certain sympathy towards someone who had been unfortunate enough to be endowed with a weak character, and smiling up at Stanley, she said: 'I would like to visit your home very much.'

'I'll be looking forward to that day, then,' he smiled, releasing her hands and climbing into his car. 'Cheerio.'

Jennifer waved him off, but her hand fell swiftly to her side moments later when a mocking voice behind her remarked, 'Poor Stanley. Someone should really warn him that he's wasting his time.'

'I wouldn't do that, if I were you, Mr Maynard,' she replied in a similar vein as she turned to face him. 'You might just spoil the beginnings of a beautiful friendship.'

'Friendship?' he snorted contemptuously. 'Is that what they call an intimate relationship these days?'

'When one wants to be discreet about it, yes,' she replied coolly, raising her glance from the strong brown column of his throat to face the onslaught of his eyes.

'My God, I was right!' he exploded harshly, those wide shoulders tense beneath his bush jacket. 'Women were made by the devil himself!'

Their glances became locked together in fury and something else which she could not quite define, but a familiar red sports car flashed past them moments later, and his features relaxed visibly as he turned towards the dark-haired girl who slid out of her car and tripped lightly across the gravel drive to join them.

'Hunter!' Carla's lilting voice exclaimed, and wrapping her arms about his neck she kissed him unashamedly and lingeringly on the lips. 'Darling, I've missed you!'

Amusement lurked in his glance as he looked a long way down into Carla's large, liquid-brown eyes. 'Have you?'

'You know I have,' she replied to his teasing query, and Jennifer experienced yet another stab of something she would rather not define, then Carla directed her gaze away from Hunter. 'Hello, Sister Casey. I passed Stanley on the way here. Has he become a regular visitor lately?'

'Not yet,' Hunter replied to her query before Jennifer had the opportunity to do so. 'Stanley is still hoping that

Sister Casey will allow him to become one of her . . . er . . . special friends.'

'Really?' Carla observed dryly, her eyes searching Jennifer's cool, expressionless features which hid successfully the churning anger within her. 'I can't think why anyone would want Stanley as a special friend, can you?' she asked Hunter, but her curiously speculative glance did not stray from Jennifer.

'Perhaps Sister Casey would be the best one to answer that,' Hunter flung the ball into Jennifer's court with a marked cynicism in his voice.

A cold, clinical anger sliced through her as she faced him, and her voice assumed an icy tone which surprised even herself. 'I owe no one an explanation for being civil to a member of your family, Mr Maynard. If you've misinterpreted my actions, then I can't help that, but I won't be mocked, and I won't have a degrading inference placed on the two innocent encounters I've had with your cousin.'

Having dispersed with some of her pent-up anger, she turned on her heel and headed towards the house, but Hunter's mocking voice stopped her in her tracks when she reached the steps.

'That was a superb performance, Sister Casey,' he announced, and when she turned reluctantly to face him, he added derisively, 'I didn't know you could add acting to your list of accomplishments.'

Jennifer stood as if turned to stone while the heat of humiliation stole into her cheeks. She could have tolerated that, and more, she realised afterwards, but Carla's high-pitched laugh had sliced through her composure, and she had fled into the house with inexplicable tears blurring her vision.

She could not care less what Hunter Maynard thought

of her, she told herself when she reached her room and had managed to regain control of herself. He was her temporary employer, and a man she had met barely a few weeks ago. His opinion meant nothing to her, and yet . . . Why did it hurt so much that he should treat her with such hostility and contempt?

She opened the doors leading out on to the balcony, hoping for a cool breeze to cool her face as well as her room, but the unfamiliar sound of Hunter's soft laughter drifted up towards her, and she closed the doors almost forcibly once more before she flung herself on to her bed and tried to rid herself of the feelings clamouring so madly within her; feelings which demanded to be analysed, but which she knew she dared not.

Carla's car was not there when Jennifer went down to Mrs Maynard's room later that afternoon, and when Hunter did not have tea with them, as was his usual custom, she surmised that he had gone off somewhere with Carla.

Jennifer's assumption proved incorrect, however, for Hunter arrived home an hour later in his truck, and from the cab he produced a pair of crutches which he placed against the wall beside his mother's chair.

'Dr Tremayne asked me to repeat his warning that you don't try to do too much too soon,' he addressed his mother without so much as a cursory glance in Jennifer's direction.

'Dr Tremayne fusses like an old woman,' Alice Maynard grumbled.

'He was nevertheless insistent,' Hunter told her dryly, 'and I echo his wishes.'

'Yes, yes, I'm sure you do,' his mother replied impatiently. 'Help me out of this chair so I can try these infernal crutches.'

'I would like to suggest that you leave that until after

you've had a good night's rest, Mrs Maynard,' Jennifer interrupted for the first time. 'You'll find the effort strenuous at first, and you'll need all your wits about you to adapt to walking with crutches.'

'Sister Casey is right,' Hunter acknowledged her existence for the first time. 'I suggest you take her advice.'

'What is this?' Alice Maynard demanded crossly. 'Are you both taking sides against me?'

'What I suggested was for your own good, Mrs Maynard,' Jennifer replied with calm, unmistakable sincerity.

'I know that,' her patient sighed, 'but you can't blame me for being in a hurry to get out of this contraption and on to my feet once more.'

'Be patient a little longer,' Jennifer advised, and Alice Maynard nodded grudgingly, her eyes following Hunter as he took the crutches through to her bedroom.

Jennifer's glance followed that tall, broad-shouldered frame as well, but her eyes mirrored a certain relief as her nerves slowly and painfully began to unravel themselves once more.

The following morning, while Jennifer was massaging Alice's legs and assisting her with her daily exercises, the older woman said unexpectedly, 'Tell me about your fiancé. Did you love him very much?'

Taken aback by this query, Jennifer could not at first reply, then she said quietly, 'I found in him all I ever wanted in a man.'

Alice Maynard smiled wryly. 'That still doesn't answer my question.'

'I loved him very much, yes,' Jennifer admitted reluctantly, but suddenly she had the uncomfortable feeling that she was referring to something which never existed, and she wondered vaguely why this should be so.

'You'll learn to love again,' Mrs Maynard announced knowingly, and Jennifer shook her head a little confusedly.

'I don't think so.'

'Oh, of course you will,' the older woman insisted, puffing a little from the exertion of the exercises Jennifer was putting her through. 'It will be a different kind of love, perhaps, but you'll learn to love someone again.'

Jennifer smiled inwardly. 'I should like to think I might.'

'I wish Hunter would find himself a nice girl to love; someone who would give him back his faith in women,' Alice remarked at length with a sigh. 'He's become hard over the years, and at thirty-five he's not so young any more.'

'Was there someone once?' Jennifer questioned her cautiously without looking up from her task.

'When he was in his early twenties, yes,' the older woman admitted, then she paused almost guiltily before continuing. 'She was a beautiful girl, and I think he was coming close to thinking of marriage when he discovered that he was merely one of the many men in her life. That seemed to finish him as far as women were concerned, and now he's become a crusty, boorish old bachelor.'

A glimmer of understanding lifted the shadows in Jennifer's heart, but only just a fraction as she looked up at Alice Maynard and said: 'He seems to be fond of Carla von Brandis.'

'I know.' Alice Maynard's expression became shuttered. 'I think you can help me get dressed now, then I'd like to try out those crutches, if you don't mind.'

Mrs Maynard's voice sounded abrupt, and very much like Hunter's at that moment, but Jennifer also received the impression of vague displeasure in her manner. She wondered why, but it was not her place to delve too deeply into her patient's personal affairs, and she left it at that.

CHAPTER FOUR

ALICE MAYNARD displayed a unique determination when she attacked the problem of walking with crutches. She persevered, enjoying the freedom of movement until her armpits ached, and Jennifer finally had to adopt a threatening attitude to encourage her into a chair.

'You're overdoing it, Mrs Maynard,' she accused severely.

'Nonsense!' Alice protested. 'I'm sure I could walk normally if I tried.'

'You will do no such thing!'

Alice Maynard looked up suddenly and laughed. 'You remind me of my sister when you use that tone of voice.'

'Please don't do anything silly like putting your weight on to that leg until Dr Tremayne thinks it's safe for you to do so,' Jennifer pleaded, relaxing her attitude slightly, but not entirely. 'I would be neglecting my duty if I didn't warn you of the consequences of such an action.'

'I know, I know,' Alice muttered. 'I could injure my hip and the whole process would have to be repeated from the start, but I warn you, my patience is wearing thin.'

'Your patience will be rewarded, I promise you,' Jennifer assured her, taking her arm and lowering her into a chair in the living-room.

It was a cool, cloudy day, with the promise of rain in the offing. The Swartberg mountains were shrouded in mist, and by the time Agnes served them with warm scones and tea, it was pouring outside.

'Baas Hunter won't be come for tea, Oumies Maynard,'

Agnes told Alice. 'Baas Hunter and Danny are working on the tractor in the shed.'

Hunter did not put in an appearance, in fact, until lunch time, and he left again immediately afterwards muttering something about a faulty gauge.

When the weather cleared later that afternoon, Jennifer went for a walk, and she wandered absently towards one of the outbuildings. The door stood open and, drawn by curiosity and the array of ostrich feathers displayed on a work-bench, she stepped inside, but her heart leapt into her throat when she found Hunter there, examining a bundle of white plumes which he covered up quickly with a sheet of canvas when he looked up to see her standing just inside the door.

His wide shoulders tensed as if in anger, but a peculiar little smile hovered about his mouth as he asked, 'Were you looking for me?'

A pulse was beating madly in her throat. 'No, I—I was going for a walk, and when I saw the open door I—I was curious.'

'Then let me satisfy your curiosity,' he said, gesturing vaguely with a muscled arm. 'This is the sorting room, if you haven't gathered that already, and if you're interested, I'll show you around.'

Jennifer felt very much like an intruder, and was tempted to turn tail and run, but his eyes, intent and probing, met hers, and when she found no mockery there, she decided that she could not brush aside the proverbial hand of friendship he seemed to be offering her.

'I'd like that, thank you,' she heard herself say a little breathlessly, and he gestured her towards the long work-bench on which ostrich feathers of all colours, shapes and sizes were sorted together, and neatly grouped.

'As you can see, when the birds are plucked their feathers are sorted into the various types and sizes. A chick is plucked for the first time when it's six to eight months old, and his wing feathers are called *spadonas*,' Hunter explained, pointing out the drab, mottled feathers of the young birds, then he picked up a neat bundle and held it out towards her. 'You'll notice that the wing feathers of all the birds are clipped, and the quills are pulled out about two months later when they're ripe and dry.'

'Isn't it painful?'

'Not at all,' he said abruptly, then he continued his informative explanation. 'The smaller feathers are, of course, used for feather dusters, but the larger ones are used mostly for millinery purposes.' He picked up a bundle of large white feathers and ran an expert hand almost caressingly over them. 'These are the selected primes, naturally. The white plumes of the male bird are the most sought after in Europe and other countries, but the hen has an equally beautiful wing feather.'

Hunter proved the latter by showing her a white wing feather with the drab colour of the hen clearly visible around the outer edges, only it no longer looked drab, it looked remarkably beautiful, and she said as much.

'You can trace a hen by the markings in her wing feathers,' Hunter told her as he handed her the feather and watched her run her hand lightly over it. 'This hen will yield the same markings each time she's clipped, and each hen's markings are different.'

'Like fingerprints?' she questioned, intensely aware of his large, muscular body standing close beside her.

'Something like that.' His lips twitched slightly, then he moved away from her to fetch a bundle of feathers further down the table. 'After about fifteen years the quality of the plumage decreases, as you can see here, for instance,' he said, demonstrating his point by indicating the tatty appearance of the feathers in his hands.

'What happens then?'

'The birds are slaughtered for their meat, and the skin is used for the manufacture of handbags, shoes, and so forth.'

'I think that's terrible!' Jennifer exclaimed with a grimace when she thought of those graceful birds being used for that purpose, then she caught sight of a hooked stick leaning against the opposite wall. 'What's that?'

'This,' he said, taking the stick and holding it in his large, perfectly shaped hands for her inspection, 'is what is commonly called a *vangstok*. The ostriches are driven into a small enclosure, then they're caught individually by slipping this hook around their necks and led into a triangular box, where they're masked with a sock to keep them docile while they're clipped and plucked.'

She was not looking at the *vangstok* now, but at those large capable-looking hands. For some obscure reason she was recalling the strange sensations aroused by their light touch, and she said in nervous haste, 'I must get back to the house.'

'I have something else to show you,' he said, taking her arm in a firm grip as he placed the hooked stick against the wall where he had found it, then he ushered her from that building into another where a hatch of chicks were huddled together in a partitioned-off section of the incubator room. 'These chicks hatched out yesterday,' he explained.

The heads and necks of the chicks were speckled and striped, and the down on their bodies looked unimpressively like dried grass, but they were nevertheless adorable.

'May I hold one?' she asked, and it looked for a moment as if he would refuse her request, then he scooped up one of the chicks and placed it in her waiting hands. She was surprised to discover that the chick was amazingly docile, while the down was incredibly soft to the touch, and she felt strangely like a child experiencing something new and exciting.

The chick exchanged hands once more a few minutes later, and as his frowning glance travelled over her, Hunter said: 'The chick has dirtied your overall.'

'That doesn't matter,' she laughed, removing the excess dirt from her white overall with a handkerchief, but when she glanced up at him she found no answering smile on his lips. 'Thanks for showing me around,' she said self-consciously now, and his eyebrows rose a fraction.

'You found it interesting?'

'Very much,' she assured him calmly, but there was something about him that set her nerves jangling; an indefinable something that flashed an urgent warning through her brain, and her voice was shaky when she muttered, 'I—I must go.'

She backed away from him nervously, but her heel kicked against something, and she lost her balance. Strong hands shot out to steady her, and the next instant she was crushed against the hard wall of his chest with his mouth taking advantage of her lips which had parted to utter a startled cry.

Shock numbed her brain and retarded her initial reactions to this unexpected invasion of her mouth, then a strange, throbbing sensation took possession of her, draining away all thoughts of resistance, and leaving her weak and pliant in his arms. She had been kissed before, but never like this, and even though her sluggish brain warned against it, her lips responded with a will of their own to the sensual exploration of Hunter's hard mouth.

Her body relaxed against his, finding enjoyment in the muscled thighs against her own, but the next instant she was set aside, and the strange magic ended as his harsh voice sliced chillingly through the warmth which had invaded her heart.

'You've got what you came looking for, and now you may go, Sister Casey.'

Jennifer felt too stupefied to react at first, but understanding finally dawned, and humiliation sent a wave of heat surging through her trembling body.

'You're an insufferable brute!' she accused, her hazel eyes flashing sparks of mingled pain and anger. 'I should have guessed that your friendliness would have a sting to it, but like a fool I believed you were willing to forget your prejudiced feelings towards me.'

'Is it an apology you want, or more of the same treatment?' he demanded, cynicism in every hard line of his face as he stepped towards her, and she backed away, clenching her shaking hands at her sides.

'I never thought I'd ever come this close to hating anyone, but you're certainly making it very easy for me to hate you, Mr Maynard.'

'Are you peeved because I haven't taken the time to lure you into my bed?'

Jennifer flinched as if he had struck her, and her voice had a husky quality to it as she said fiercely, 'You disgust me!'

'I may disgust you, but I'm willing to bet that you enjoyed my kisses a moment ago,' he mocked her ruthlessly and, unable to take more, she turned and fled with the sound of his mocking laughter ringing hatefully in her ears.

Her head was throbbing painfully when she reached the house, but it was nothing compared to the stabbing agony in her heart. She had done nothing to deserve Hunter's scandalous insinuations, but the most dreadful part of it all was that she could do nothing to prove how wrong he was about her. He would never believe her. Why should he? Why, moreover, should she bother? He cared nothing for her, and she cared——! She pulled herself up sharply, mentally reprimanding herself, but those last two words rang through her mind with a force that made her face the agonising truth whether she wanted to, or not. *She cared*!

Colin's boyishly endearing face had faded from her mind during these past weeks, to be replaced by the mocking, cynical, and often cruel features of a man who had, only moments ago, shown how much he despised her. She would get over it, no doubt, as she had got over Colin's death, but she had a dreadful feeling that this time the scars would go very much deeper.

'Jennifer?' Alice Maynard's voice halted her in her flight across the spacious hall, and she retraced her steps rather reluctantly to join her patient in the living-room. 'Why are you crying?'

'I'm not——' Jennifer paused abruptly when her fingers brushed against her cheeks to find them surprisingly damp, and unable to explain the reason for her tears, she said vaguely, 'I'm just being silly, that's all.'

'It's Hunter, isn't it?'

Alice was much too shrewd for comfort, and knowing the futility of being evasive, Jennifer nodded and sat down heavily in the nearest chair.

'Perhaps I was wrong to accept this job when he was so strongly opposed to having me here,' she found herself trying to make excuses for him.

'Nonsense!' Alice contradicted her sharply. 'It was for me to say whether I wanted you or not, and I wouldn't have had anyone else.'

A warmth surged into Jennifer's cold heart, and she smiled shakily. 'You're very kind, Mrs Maynard, but——'

'I won't have you feeling guilty about being here, is that understood?' Alice interrupted firmly, but gently, and Jennifer pulled herself together with an effort.

'I understand perfectly, Mrs Maynard.'

Hunter did not come in to dinner that evening, and neither did he join them for breakfast the following morning, but he came in afterwards and pressed a bundle of white plumes into his mother's hands.

'I thought this might interest you,' he announced, and only then did Alice and Jennifer notice the two black spots, perfectly spaced, near the tip of the feathers. 'It's unusual, isn't it?' Hunter remarked.

'Very unusual,' his mother agreed, examining the feathers more closely. 'Where did you get this?'

'It's from one of the young birds which was plucked yesterday morning,' he explained, smiling twistedly. 'If this was the nineteen-twenties then this bird's plumage would have amounted to an unearthly sum of money, but in this day and age it's considered as a freak.'

'Why should it be considered a freak?' Jennifer asked before she could prevent herself, and those blue eyes focussed on her for the first time that morning with a coldness that pierced right through her heart.

'Since the feather industry discovered the art of dyeing the white male plumes any colour they wished, feathers such as these lost their intrinsic value,' he explained with an unmistakable hint of impatience in his voice at her ignorance, and she felt herself colouring beneath his direct gaze.

'What are you going to do with this?' Alice asked, gesturing with the spotted plumes, and Hunter shrugged carelessly.

'I might make something out of it privately, or I might just send it along to the K.K.L. to do with as they please,' he said, and before Jennifer could formulate the question in her mind, Hunter turned to her once more and explained with a great deal of sarcasm, 'K.K.L. stands for Klein Karoo Landbouko öperasie. It's a co-operative society to which all ostrich farmers have to send their produce to be auctioned, or slaughtered.'

Alice Maynard frowned up at her son, but before she could say anything, Jennifer remarked with equal sarcasm, 'Thanks for the information.'

His mouth tightened ominously, but he turned without a word and strode from the room, leaving Alice and Jennifer to examine the feathers at their leisure.

'Oumies Maynard? Where did Oumies get that?' Agnes demanded in surprise when she came in to clear away the breakfast dishes, and when they glanced up at her she pointed towards the feathers Alice held in her hands. Alice explained that it came from one of Hunter's young birds, and Agnes' eyes widened with a certain excitement. 'Do you know what that means, *Oumies*?' she asked Alice Maynard.

'Am I going to have to listen to one of your strange beliefs again, Agnes?' Mrs Maynard sighed with a humorous twinkle in her eyes.

'*Oumies*!' Agnes continued excitedly. 'Before this year ends Baas Hunter is going to be married. You'll see, *Oumies*.'

It felt as though a cold hand was clutching Jennifer's heart, the fingers squeezing until it ached, and it was only when Agnes had returned to the kitchen that Alice Maynard stirred in her chair.

'I sincerely hope she's right, and I can only pray that Hunter makes a sensible choice,' Alice announced with a severe look on her face as she levered herself up on to her crutches and left the room.

The spotted plumes remained behind on the table, and Jennifer picked them up idly to study them more closely. On each feather, in precisely the same place, two spots like black eyes in a white face stared back at her, and she was fingering them lightly, almost reverently, when Agnes returned to the breakfast-room to clear the table.

'What's so special about these feathers, Agnes?' she could not prevent herself from asking, and Agnes' face lit up with importance.

'Nonnie Jennifer, I know of two men who bred an ostrich with markings like this one. The one man was young, and the other was Oumies Maynard's age, and they were both married before that year came to an end.'

'Don't you think you've become superstitious as a result of an unusual coincidence?'

'Call it what you like, *nonnie*,' Agnes shrugged, then she waved her finger almost admonishingly at Jennifer. 'You will see that I am right. I'm always right about these things.'

Those cold fingers which were wrapped around Jennifer's heart seemed to squeeze harder and, leaving the bundle of plumes on the table where Hunter would find them, she went in search of Alice Maynard.

No matter how much Jennifer tried, she could not forget Agnes' prediction that morning. It was ridiculous, of course, to think so much about it, but she could not help herself. What if Agnes was right, and what if the woman he chose to marry was Carla von Brandis? It was none of her business, really, whom he chose to marry, but it left her with an achingly empty feeling she could not rid herself of.

Hunter's cousin arrived at Vogelsvlei that day just as they were lingering over a cup of tea at the luncheon table, and Alice was the first to recover from her surprise to say, 'You've arrived just too late to have lunch with us, Stanley.'

'I've had something to eat, Aunt Alice,' he said quickly and, looking as though he did not quite know what to do with his hands, he added: 'I came, actually, to ask if you could spare Jennifer for this afternoon.'

'Is something wrong out at Featherstone?' Alice asked at once.

'Nothing is wrong, Aunt Alice,' Stanley smiled a little selfconsciously. 'I'd like Jennifer to spend the afternoon with us, that's all.'

Alice Maynard hesitated momentarily, then she smiled with a peculiar sparkle in her eyes. 'You should ask Jennifer that, shouldn't you?'

Stanley turned his enquiring glance on Jennifer and asked, 'Will you come?'

Three pairs of eyes were suddenly focussed on Jennifer, but she was conscious, most of all, of the derisive mockery in Hunter's glance as it met hers and, disconcerted, she looked away again.

'Well, I . . .' she began hesitantly, bordering on a refusal, but something made her decide against it and, glancing at the woman seated opposite her, she asked resolutely, 'Will you manage without me, Mrs Maynard?'

'Of course I'll manage,' she replied at once and, taking her at her word, Jennifer glanced up at Stanley.

'When did you want to leave?'

'At once, if you don't mind.'

'I'll just go upstairs and change,' Jennifer nodded and, excusing herself from the table, she went up to her room.

She did not feel like going out to Featherstone at all, she admitted to herself, and neither had she any desire to strike up a closer relationship with Stanley, but Hunter's manner had driven her to accept Stanley's invitation. She was angry with herself for allowing herself to be enveigled into this position because of Hunter's attitude, but there was nothing she could do now to alter the decision she had made. She was going out to Featherstone with Stanley, and that was that.

After wearing white every day for the past few weeks, she felt good slipping into an emerald green dress of fine silk which clung softly to her slender figure. She loosened her hair from its confining chignon, and after brushing it vigorously until it shone she decided to leave it hanging loose on to her shoulders.

'Well, well, well,' Hunter remarked mockingly when she encountered him in the passage just outside her room a few minutes later, and his glance was almost an insult as it travelled with slow deliberation from her shining head down to her small, sandalled feet. 'So Stanley is going to receive the full treatment, is he?'

Jennifer stiffened, her veiled eyes taking in the height and breath of the man barring her way. 'I don't know what you're talking about.'

'No, of course you don't. You're an innocent little girl going out on her first party.'

His mockery was uncalled for, but she decided to ignore it as she said coldly, 'Let me pass, please.'

'In a minute.' She stepped back as he advanced towards her, and the next instant she was imprisoned against the wall when he placed a hand on either side of her. The clean male smell of him stirred her senses, and a tell-tale pulse jerked in her throat when she looked up into his angry eyes.

'Don't play around too much with Stanley,' Hunter warned in a grating voice. 'He's really a trusting soul, and he might just take you seriously.'

'I think he's old enough to take care of himself, don't you?' she remarked defiantly, but the ominous tightening of his jaw made her heart jerk with fear.

'There's not much love lost between my cousin and myself, as you must have gathered by now, but I wouldn't like to see him hurt.'

'What makes you think I want to hurt him?' she demanded incredulously.

'You're out looking for excitement, Sister Casey, and he's the only one around who's gullible enough to fall for your beguiling little ways.'

Jennifer was not quite sure whether to laugh or cry, but the question was resolved when anger took over, and she asked with chilling politeness, 'Have you quite finished?'

'Not quite,' Hunter smiled dangerously. 'I'd like to give you something to take along with you to Featherstone.'

She received no warning as to his intentions, and she was totally defenceless when she found herself trapped between Hunter and the wall behind her. His hard mouth swooped down on to hers and drew an involuntary response from her even as his hands roamed insultingly over her taut body. She tried to push him away with her hands flat against his hard chest, but he was as immovable as a rock, and he did not stop until she trembled with something close to desire at the sensual pressure of his fingers through the fine silk at her breasts.

'It's a good thing you're wearing non-smudgeable lipstick, isn't it?' he laughed harshly when he released her.

'You're despicable!' she hissed up at him, trying desperately to control her pulse rate and to regain what little composure she still had left.

'Don't dawdle on your way down,' he mocked her ruthlessly. 'Stanley's becoming rather impatient in his desire to get his hands on your worthless body.'

He could not have inflicted more pain if he had struck her, and she recoiled from him, the blood draining slowly from her face to leave her deathly pale. She tried to speak, but couldn't, and she turned instead without a word to join Stanley on the verandah where he was waiting for her. For some obscure reason Hunter had reduced her to feeling cheap and dirty, and the experience had left her with the taste of bitterness in her mouth.

'I'm going now, Mrs Maynard,' she said to the woman seated in her favourite cane chair on the cool verrandah.

'Enjoy yourself, my dear,' Alice smiled up at her, then her glance sharpened. 'You look rather pale, Jennifer. Is something wrong?'

'It must be the heat,' Jennifer brushed aside her query. 'I shan't be back till late this afternoon.'

'Aunt Alice was right,' Stanley remarked, observing her closely when she sat beside him in his car. 'You do look quite pale.'

'I'll be all right in a minute,' she insisted, wishing he would start the car and drive away from Vogelsvlei.

'Did something happen?' he persisted with concern. 'Something to upset you, perhaps?'

Jennifer sighed inwardly and turned towards him in her seat to ask sharply, 'Are you taking me out to Featherstone, or are we going to sit here all afternoon discussing my appearance?'

'All right, I won't pry,' Stanley nodded agreeably, 'but it wouldn't surprise me at all if Hunter hasn't something to do with it. His mother and young Carla are the only women to escape the sharp edge of his tongue.'

His expression was tight-lipped as he started the car and drove away from Vogelsvlei, and it was some minutes before Jennifer remarked thoughtfully, 'One can't really blame him for not speaking harshly to Carla. She's very beautiful.'

'She's also a little vixen,' Stanley returned at once. 'And Hunter will be getting just what he deserves the day he marries her.'

Agnes' prediction sprang to the surface of her mind once more, but this time with stinging clarity as she asked tentatively, 'Are they going to be married?'

'So Carla says.'

Jennifer's hands tightened almost convulsively in her lap. 'What does Hunter say about it?'

'Hunter isn't a man who talks about himself, and neither does he tolerate being questioned about his personal life.'

'You know him well, though,' she pursued the topic with care. 'Would you say that he's in love with Carla?'

'Love?' Stanley snorted disparagingly. 'Hunter has a heart of stone, my dear Jennifer. He has all the natural desires and instincts of a man, but when it comes to love he's like a slab of lifeless concrete.' He laughed harshly. 'He'll take what he can get from a woman, but when she has nothing more to give he'll drop her flat.'

Inwardly shocked by his remark, but outwardly calm, she said: 'You make him sound quite inhuman.'

'And isn't he just that?' Stanley demanded, glancing at her swiftly before returning his attention to the road.

'Sometimes, yes, but——'

'But what?' he demanded sharply, swerving the car off the road unexpectedly, and switching off the engine before he swung round in his seat to face her with a suspicious gleam in his eyes. 'Don't tell me you have been silly enough to fall in love with Hunter?'

'Don't be ridiculous!' she denied crossly, shutting her mind to that taunting little voice that called her a liar. 'I can't stand him most of the time,' she added almost vehemently.

'Well, that's a relief anyway,' Stanley sighed, capturing one of her hands. 'It gets rather tiring to have to compete with my cousin all the time.'

'Stanley . . .' she began nervously, then she took a firm grip on her flagging courage and said gently but firmly, 'There's no question of competition where I'm concerned. I would like to enjoy your company, but I can't do that if you're going to read something more into our friendship than I'm prepared to give.'

His crestfallen expression was a clear indication that she had been correct in her assumption, but he recovered himself swiftly and nodded agreeably. 'I appreciate your honesty, Jennifer.'

He started the car again and drove on in silence; a silence during which Jennifer's mind went back towards the early part of their conversation.

Carla von Brandis had told Stanley that she and Hunter were to be married. Could she be believed, or was it merely wishful thinking which had driven her to impart this information? Jennifer wondered about it, but, if she had to judge, she would say that Carla had quite possibly spoken the truth. Hunter had never once shown any sign of displeasure in Carla's company, and neither did he reject her cloying manner, so what reason would there be for Carla to lie? It was a painful thought, but one Jennifer would have to accept. It was quite possible, of course, that Hunter was fond of Carla in his fashion, and if Agnes' prediction should come true, then Hunter and Carla would be married before the end of the year.

'Featherstone is just beyond those trees,' Stanley's voice interrupted her thoughts, and it was with pain-filled eyes that she glanced in the direction he was indicating.

CHAPTER FIVE

FEATHERSTONE'S homestead was not as impressive as Vogelsvlei's, but it possessed a charm of its own with its gables and turrets and wide, trellised verandah. The interior had none of the polished splendour which Jennifer had encountered in Alice Maynard's home, but it had a comfortable, lived-in atmosphere that appealed a great deal to her.

'Jennifer!' Kate Maynard exclaimed, smiling broadly as she welcomed Jennifer into her home. 'How nice to have you here at last as our guest.'

'It's very nice to be here, Mrs Maynard,' Jennifer replied with polite sincerity.

'How is Alice?'

'She's very much better.'

'I believe she's walking on crutches now.'

'That's quite correct,' Jennifer acknowledged. 'It won't be long now before she'll walk with the aid of a stick only, judging by the way she's progressing.'

'I hope that doesn't mean you will be leaving Oudtshoorn soon?' Stanley asked quickly.

'I'm afraid it does,' Jennifer nodded, avoiding those hungry eyes. 'I doubt if I shall be here for another three weeks.'

Mother and son exchanged quick glances, then Kate said: 'I'd be delighted if you would consider spending a few weeks here with us before returning to Cape Town, Jennifer.'

'It's kind of you to suggest it, Mrs Maynard,' Jennifer replied politely, 'but I'm afraid I shall have to return to Cape Town at once.'

'That's a pity,' Kate frowned, 'but you could always come for a holiday, I suppose.'

'You will consider that, won't you, Jennifer?' Stanley asked with an eagerness she could not avoid noticing, and quite suddenly she pitied him.

'Yes, of course,' she agreed, hiding her initial reluctance, 'and thank you very much for the invitation.'

A smile lit up his lean face and, glancing at his mother, he said: 'What about something long and cool to drink?'

'That's an excellent idea,' Kate replied at once. 'I'll bring it out into the garden.'

Contrary to what Jennifer had hoped, she found herself alone with Stanley for most of the afternoon, but her initial wariness soon vanished. Keeping in mind what she had told him on the way to Featherstone, he never once stepped over the line of friendship, and she appreciated this. He was, she found, relaxing to be with, and often amusing as he kept her entertained with beliefs and anecdotes from the past during the ostrich feather boom, and she learnt, too, that his father had been killed by one of his own infuriated ostriches. Had it been due to carelessness? Jennifer wondered briefly, recalling Alice's remarks concerning her late brother-in-law.

'You like the view of the Outeniqua mountains?' Stanley queried as he intercepted her glance while they strolled back towards the house from one of the nearby grazing camps, and when she nodded, he said: 'Outeniqua means 'little brown men with skin bags of honey', and naturally it's referring to the Bushmen.' His hand on her arm drew her to a halt. 'Did you know that an ostrich eggshell is one of the most valued possessions of the nomadic Bushmen of the Kalahari?'

Jennifer narrowed her eyes against the glare of the sun as she glanced up at him and shook her head. 'I didn't know, but I presume they use them for storing water. How on earth do they prevent the water from spilling out, though?'

'They seal the opening with beeswax,' he explained, and as he removed his hand from his trouser pocket to gesture expressively, something fell to the ground at their feet.

It was a gold chain and, with a muttered oath, he bent down quickly to retrieve it, but not before Jennifer had glimpsed the name, twisted in fine gold wire, attached to the chain.

Carla. There was only one girl by that name that Jennifer knew of, but what was her chain doing in this man's trouser pocket?

Her enquiring glance met Stanley's, but he looked away with a measure of discomfort and mumbled, 'Shall we return to the house?'

'I think so,' Jennifer nodded. 'It's also time I returned to Vogelsvlei.'

'But it's still early,' Stanley protested, fully recovered now after that moment of awkwardness.

'No, it's not,' she contradicted, glancing at her wrist watch. 'It's a quarter past four, and Mrs Maynard likes to wash and change before dinner in the evenings.'

'It took me so long to get you here that I feel disinclined to let you go,' Stanley teased, then he placed his hand beneath her elbow as they approached the house. 'You will come again, won't you, Jennifer?'

'If I'm invited, yes.'

His smile broadened. 'I shall issue you with a daily invitation.'

'Don't be silly,' she laughed, but her expression sobered when she thought of the perplexing incident she had witnessed moments ago. Stanley's eyes were watchful, almost wary and, shedding her thoughts, she said abruptly, 'I'd like to pay my respects to your mother, then you really must take me back to Vogelsvlei.'

'Your wish is my command,' he bowed slightly in an attempt at lightheartedness, but there was a new wariness in his manner, and Jennifer was beginning to suspect the cause of it.

That night, alone in her room, she allowed her thoughts to dwell on what had occurred at Featherstone that afternoon. For some reason, she knew not what, Stanley carried Carla's chain around with him in his pocket. He could, of course, have picked it up with the intention of returning it to her, but if he had obtained it by innocent means, then why had he not offered her some sort of explanation instead of remaining silent and obviously disturbed by what he knew she had seen? There was only one other explanation Jennifer could find for Carla's chain being in Stanley's possession. Carla must have given it to him, and for some or other reason he cherished it to such an extent that he carried it with him constantly.

It didn't make sense, she decided at last. None of it made any sense! Carla was, quite obviously, setting her cap at Hunter, yet Stanley walked around with one of her personal trinkets in his pocket. Was she placing too much significance on what she had seen? Jennifer wondered. Or was Carla playing a double game?

Jennifer felt almost feverish at the thought of what it would do to Hunter if her suspicions were correct. He had suffered a woman's treachery once before, but what would it do to him if he encountered it once again from someone he had thought he could trust?

She tightened the belt of her dressing-gown about her waist, and stepped out on to the balcony to draw the cool, fresh air deep into her lungs. The breeze caressed her throbbing temples, and she closed her eyes for a moment as she leaned against one of the pillars supporting the railings.

A step on the gravel below her made her stare searchingly into the darkness, but she could see no one until the glowing tip of a cigarette made her realise that Hunter was standing below her, staring out across the garden. He seldom smoked except when he was disturbed, and this was obviously one of those moments. She could see him now; a tall, dark shadow moving across the path, the gravel crunching beneath his feet, and his harsh features visible for a moment when he drew hard on his cigarette once more. He turned to glance up at the house, and she stepped back hastily into the shadows, her heart leaping uncomfortably into her throat at the thought that he might have seen her, but he turned away and walked farther into the shadows.

She watched him go with an aching tenderness and a concern she had felt for no one before. It was ridiculous, of course. He would despise her tender feelings, just as he would mock her concern, and she would rather suffer his insults than have him suspect the emotions he had awakened in her.

With a sigh on her lips she turned away and, closing the doors behind her, she went to bed, but it was a long time before she went to sleep. It was not until she heard Hunter's heavy step in the passage, in fact, that she gained a certain amount of peace within herself, and her eyelids drooped some minutes later.

Alice Maynard and Jennifer were having tea out on the shady verandah the following morning when Carla's red car sped towards the house and came to a halt below the steps with its usual crunching of tyres on the gravel.

'Hello there!' Carla greeted airily as she bounced up the steps. 'Where's Hunter?'

'He's busy somewhere on the farm,' Alice replied stiffly as she observed the young girl's quivering impatience.

'But he knew I'd be calling round this morning,' Carla pouted angrily.

'My dear child, Hunter is far too busy to sit around waiting for you.'

Carla's glowering glance met Alice's. 'I never said I expected him to sit around and wait for me, Mrs Maynard, but I——'

'Why don't you find yourself something to do?' Alice interrupted, her eyes unexpectedly hard. 'You've had a good education, and you shouldn't have any difficulty finding yourself a job somewhere.'

A look of distaste flashed across Carla's beautiful face. 'There's no necessity for me to work.'

'So you spend your time keeping others out of theirs,' Alice Maynard remarked cuttingly, and turning to Jennifer she said: 'Help me up, please. I think I'd like to lie down for a while.'

The atmosphere was heavy with animosity as Jennifer assisted Alice to her feet and handed her her crutches. This was the first time she had ever witnessed a clash of sorts between Carla and Alice, but she could not deny that the younger girl's manner had been a source of irritation to her as well.

'You know,' Carla scowled when they were alone on the verandah, 'one of the first things I'll do when Hunter and I are married is to put that old woman out of this house!'

A tremor of shock rippled through Jennifer, but it was followed by a vicious stab of pain. Carla had made it sound as if her marriage to Hunter was something quite definite, but it was also the latter part of her statement that disturbed Jennifer, and she said anxiously, 'You can't do that! You can't turn Mrs Maynard out of her own home.'

'I can, you know,' Carla insisted, her sensuous mouth thinning. 'She's been a thorn in my side for much too long.'

'I don't think Hunter will agree with you on this issue,' Jennifer remarked with a measure of distaste.

'I always get what I want,' Carla smiled confidently, 'and Hunter will do whatever I ask him to.'

Jennifer considered Carla's statement in thoughtful silence, but somehow she could not imagine Hunter going weak in the knees at a command from the young Carla, and she shook her head as she said contemplatively, 'I doubt it.'

'What do you doubt, Sister Casey?' Hunter demanded, and she looked up sharply to see him negotiate the steps on to the verandah in two lithe strides, and his presence, as always, quickened her pulse rate and alerted her to his virile masculinity.

'Darling!' Carla intervened, leaping to her feet to drap herself against his large frame. 'I thought you'd never come!'

He afforded Carla a brief, smiling glance before he returned his attention to Jennifer, who had managed, at last, to rise a little shakily to her feet. 'You haven't answered my question, Sister Casey.'

To answer his question she would have to reveal the discussion she had had with Carla and, glancing helplessly at the girl, she said haltingly, 'I—well, I——'

'What she was saying, darling, was that she doubted whether you would be home before lunch,' Carla intervened, choosing a devious method to come to Jennifer's rescue. 'Silly of her, wasn't it, because here you are.'

'Very silly of her, yes, and rather presumptuous,' Hunter agreed, his cold eyes never leaving Jennifer's.

'To tell the truth, Hunter, I think she was hoping that I'd leave without seeing you,' Carla continued, her smile sweet, but her glance challenging as it met Jennifer's.

'I was hoping no such thing, and you know it,' Jennifer replied with a coolness that surprised even herself, but her cheeks were flaming with indignation and anger.

'Then why are you blushing?' Carla persisted cleverly. 'Guilty conscience?'

Jennifer was momentarily at a loss for words. She was conscious only of the proud tilt of Hunter's dark head, of the savage expression in his eyes, and the blue shirt that seemed to stretch too tightly across the width of his powerful shoulders. Faded blue denims hugged lean hips and muscular thighs, and when her senses began to respond to his physical appearance, she hastily turned her attention back to the girl at his side.

'My conscience is clear, Carla,' she managed stiffly, 'but I most certainly wouldn't want yours.'

Hunter could make of that what he liked, she decided as she stepped past them and entered the house. If he was going to make a fool of himself over a girl as fickle as the one he had been involved with before, then it was entirely his own business, but—oh, God, she didn't want him to be hurt again, and she was totally powerless to prevent it.

'Are you not feeling well, Mrs Maynard?' Jennifer asked when she entered Alice's bedroom to find her lying on her bed with an expression on her face which was a mixture of annoyance and possible pain. 'Would you like me to massage your leg for you?'

Alice shook her head and patted the space on the bed beside her. 'Sit down here and talk to me.'

'What's upset you?' Jennifer asked at length when she was seated on the bed beside Hunter's mother.

'It's not *what*, but *whom*, my dear,' Alice replied agitatedly. 'I've never been able to tolerate Carla, and I seem to be able to tolerate her even less now.'

Jennifer smiled, but her amusement was tinged with fear. 'Has Agnes' prediction something to do with the way you feel?'

'You're so right, it has,' Alice sighed, drawing herself up against the pillows. 'I don't know what I'll do, Jennifer, if Hunter should decide to marry that girl.'

'You should credit him with more sense than to make a fool of himself twice,' she reprimanded the woman lying staring up at her, but the reprimand was also intended for herself.

'I'd like to, but I've been watching them together lately,' Alice confessed with a measure of distaste. 'He's known Carla since she was a child, and she's always seemed to amuse him in some way, but lately he's actually been encouraging her.'

Fear had a stranglehold on Jennifer's throat as she asked, 'Encouraging her in what way, Mrs Maynard?'

'Well, just look how he allows her to claw at him and kiss him in public. In the past he used to put her in her place and hold her at arm's length, but lately——' Alice Maynard snorted angrily. 'I don't know what's got into him, and if he's not careful he's going to land himself in a great deal of unhappiness once again.'

'Perhaps you're worrying unnecessarily,' Jennifer offered faintly.

'Am I, Jennifer?' Their glances met and held until Jennifer was forced to look away. 'You see, you can't truthfully say that I'm troubled unnecessarily, and that fickle little witch seems to be able to do with him just as she likes these days.'

It was with this troubling thought that Jennifer somehow managed to get through the rest of the day, and with it came the memory of Carla's gold chain in Stanley's possession. What *did* it mean?

A few days later she had cause to confront Hunter in his study after she had settled Alice Maynard for the night, and her tentative knock on the door was followed by an abrupt command to enter.

Jennifer swallowed nervously and went in, closing the door quietly behind her, then she faced him across the wide expanse of his desk, her eyes drawn by his compelling glance.

'May I speak with you for a moment?'

'Is it important?' he barked at her, almost succeeding in stripping her of her composure which had become rather fragile since her arrival at Vogelsvlei.

'Dr. Tremayne would like to see your mother at the hospital tomorrow morning, and I wondered if you would object if I took her in my Fiat.'

His dark brows met in a frown. 'What time does she have to be at the hospital?'

'Ten-thirty.'

'I'll take you,' he came to an abrupt decision, tapping his fingers impatiently on the desk blotter.

'In your truck?' she asked, having visions of herself being deposited out in the open on the back of the dusty four-wheel-drive vehicle he used constantly about the farm.

'In my car,' his cutting voice sliced into her thoughts, then he added mockingly, 'I do have one, you know.'

Her cheeks grew pink under his mocking stare. 'I'm sorry.'

'We'll leave at ten, if that will suit you both.'

There was a note of dismissal in his voice, and she said hastily, 'That would be fine, thank you.'

'I suppose you're anxious to see Mike Hoffman again,' his rasping voice stopped her on her way to the door, and she turned to face him once more, controlled anger replacing her initial surprise.

'I can't deny that it would be nice seeing him again. We were great friends once,' she replied, unable to prevent herself from deliberately adding fuel to the fire of his suspicions. She knew that she had succeeded by the sardonic expression which had settled on his hard features, and she despised herself for it.

'You're hoping, I suppose, that you could pick up where you left off all that time ago?'

'Yes, of course.'

His mouth tightened as he rose from behind his desk. 'You have no shame, have you?'

'I've never done anything I need be ashamed of,' she replied wearily, knowing that her truthful replies were being twisted out of proportion to suit his own purpose.

'That's exactly what I said,' he replied harshly, his eyes burning their way down the length of her with disgusting insolence. 'You have no shame because you don't consider your actions shameful.'

She swallowed down the pain that rose in her throat, and said huskily, 'You're accusing me of being something that I'm not, and never have been.'

'What else am I to think when you tell me that you and Mike Hoffman were once such great friends?' he demanded, thrusting his clenched fists into the pockets of his corded pants and glaring at her as if she were something to be despised. 'Mike has made no secret of the fact that all the women who have gone through his hands have at some time or another succumbed sufficiently to his charms to be lured into his bed.'

There was an awful silence while her colour came and went. It was typical of Mike to pass on such intimate information about himself. Some might call it boasting, but to Mike it simply meant being truthful, and when she found her voice at last, she said huskily, 'All but one, Mr Maynard.'

'You surely don't expect me to believe that, do you?' he demanded, his eyes narrowed slits of fire that seemed to be scorching her very soul.

'You can believe what you like,' she finally shrugged. 'I didn't come here to discuss my personal life with you, but to arrange for your mother to get to the hospital tomorrow, and now that that's settled, I'll wish you goodnight.'

'Just a minute.' Hunter moved with breathtaking speed to place a restraining hand of steel on the door which she was about to open, and his menacing nearness made her nerve ends quiver. 'I would like to make one thing very clear to you. You will leave Vogelsvlei the moment Dr Tremayne gives the signal that my mother is capable of taking care of herself.'

She lowered her gold-tipped lashes to veil the pain in her eyes. 'In one way or another, Mr Maynard, you've made that abundantly clear right from the first moment we met, and it will be my pleasure to accommodate you in that respect.'

'Get out!' he thundered, flinging the door wide.

'With pleasure, just don't burst a blood vessel,' she replied with heavy sarcasm, but instead of allowing her to leave as he had instructed, one large hand closed about her aching throat, and it exerted just enough pressure so that she couldn't move an inch farther.

He was suddenly so close to her that she could feel his thighs brushing against her own, and his lips were drawn back in anger against strong white teeth. She was afraid, but she dared not show it, although she was certain that he must feel the rapid beat of her pulse beneath his restricting fingers.

'I shall not tolerate your insolence for very much longer,' he warned thickly.

'You won't have to,' she managed to force the words past the lump in her throat, but her voice was a mere whisper.

He was breathing heavily, she could feel the rise and fall of his chest against her small breasts which were suddenly straining against the thin cotton of her overall, but what disturbed her most was the sight of his pupils enlarging to the extent that she could barely see the rim of blue surrounding them. The pressure of his hand against her throat relaxed and moved in an unconscious caress that made her senses leap in response until her entire body was filled with the aching need to know the touch of his lips and hands. Her pulses were drumming out a wild, alien message while she stared hypnotically up into those dark eyes devouring her with such ferocity, and then, surprisingly, she felt him tremble against her. With a sharp intake of breath he lowered his head, but before his lips could touch hers he thrust her from him with an exclamation of disgust.

'Get out of here before I throw you out!' he ordered harshly, and, feeling oddly bewildered and lost, she turned and walked blindly out of his study on trembling, unsteady legs.

Alone in her room, some minutes later, she tried to analyse what had happened between them, but one thing stood out as if it had been printed in bold, black letters on a snow-white sheet of paper. Hunter was not as immune to her as he would have her believe. 'He has all the desires and instincts of a man,' she recalled Stanley's words of a few days ago, and what had happened down there in his study had proved Stanley right. Hunter had shown quite clearly that her nearness had disturbed him emotionally. It had disgusted him, but it had been there all the same, and it was a strange feeling to know that she had the power, however small, to move him in this way.

This could lead nowhere, of course, and she knew that. He still despised her; perhaps much more now than before; and her chances of convincing him to the contrary were suddenly much slimmer. There was only one woman Hunter seemed to believe in implicitly, and that was Carla; Carla, who Jennifer was sure would not hesitate to lie and cheat her way into his affections, only to leave him hurt and disillusioned once again.

'Oh, damn!' Jennifer muttered, thumping her pillow repeatedly to give vent to her feelings. 'Damn Carla; damn that other woman, and damn Hunter for being so stubbornly blind to the truth when he's come face to face with it!'

Taking her aggression out on her pillow did nothing to alleviate her frustration and heartache and, not being one given to unnecessary tears, she took a cold, refreshing shower and went to bed.

Jennifer was surprised and faintly amused the following morning when she saw the large silver Mercedes parked just below the verandah steps, and she had great difficulty in avoiding Hunter's coldly cynical glance as she helped his mother from the house and into the back seat of the car. This meant, of course, that she would have to sit in front with Hunter, and at that moment she was not so sure that she wanted to be within touching distance of him. He had a devastating effect on her receptive nerves at the best of times, but, in his grey, lightweight suit, white silk shirt and matching grey tie, he made her feel rather weak in the knees. He was so tall, so strong, and those incredibly blue eyes beneath those dark brows seldom left her in peace.

The trip to Oudtshoorn was accomplished swiftly and in comfort, but Jennifer had been intensely conscious of the muscled thigh not far from her own, the strong hands resting lightly on the steering wheel, and the chiselled profile of the man seated beside her. What would he look like, she found herself wondering, if his features were to soften in tenderness?

Mike Hoffman assisted Dr Tremayne during the lengthy and thorough examination of Alice Maynard, and Jennifer remained at her side when she was wheeled to the X-ray department. This alleviated the necessity of having to sit out the time in the reception foyer with Hunter, but her thoughts somehow never strayed far from him and her heart leapt crazily when they finally emerged from the lift to find him pacing the floor restlessly.

'In another week or so you might try putting some weight on that leg, but I insist that you use a walking stick at first,' Dr Tremayne was saying.

'What nonsense!' Alice exclaimed crossly. 'I'm sure I could walk perfectly now if I tried.'

'But you're not going to try, Mrs Maynard,' Dr Tremayne warned. 'You're going to do as I say.'

'You're all a lot of bullies in the medical profession,' Alice complained.

'Now that's not true, and you know it,' Dr Tremayne protested.

'It's true,' Alice insisted. 'You've bullied me for weeks now. First you put me in that dreadful traction, then you wouldn't let me go home unless I had a qualified nurse to look after me, and now you think you can tell me when I may or may not use my own legs.'

Hunter placed a restraining hand on her shoulder. 'It's all been for your own good, Mother.'

'Yes, of course,' Alice sighed resignedly, then she glanced at Mike, who was doing his best not to smile. 'And you, young man? What do you have to say for yourself?'

Mike Hoffman suddenly radiated that familiar charm which Jennifer knew so well, and she knew, too, that he used it mostly when he was out to get something.

'I was hoping, Mrs Maynard,' Mike replied suavely, 'that you would give me the opportunity of persuading you to allow me to take Jennifer out to dinner this evening.'

'Mike!' Jennifer gasped in shocked surprise, aware suddenly of Hunter's narrowed glance resting on her person. 'You know I can't——'

'Of course you can, Jennifer,' Alice Maynard interrupted. 'You have my permission, Dr Hoffman, to take Jennifer out to dinner, but on condition that you bring her back safely to Vogelsvlei.'

'You have my word on that,' Mike bowed towards her gallantly and, after excusing himself, he winked brazenly at Jennifer and said: 'I'll call for you at six.'

'But I——'

'Why protest, Sister Casey?' Hunter murmured mockingly from his position directly behind her as she stood staring after Mike's retreating figure. 'This is what you were hoping for, isn't it?'

Helpless frustration welled up inside her, but there was nothing she could do about it with Alice Maynard and Dr Tremayne looking on. They had fortunately not heard Hunter's remark, and Jennifer tried to behave as if nothing had happened, but Hunter's accusations, although unspoken, were almost tangible.

It was Dr Tremayne who broke the awkward little silence by announcing, 'I'm going to make an appointment for you to see a specialist in Port Elizabeth.'

'What on earth do I have to see a specialist for?' Alice demanded agitatedly. 'I'm perfectly happy with what you've done for me.'

'I'm very glad to hear that you're satisfied even though you accused me of being a bully a few moments ago,' Dr Tremayne teased. 'However, *I'm* the one who won't be entirely satisfied until a specialist has given you a thorough examination once more.'

'This is just an added nuisance,' Alice protested, but Dr Tremayne had already turned to speak to Hunter.

'If you could collect the X-rays tomorrow afternoon, then I should be able to give you the date and time of Mrs Maynard's appointment, and it would save time if you took the X-rays along with you.'

Hunter nodded with obvious impatience, and a few minutes later he was driving them back to Vogelsvlei in stony silence. At the luncheon table he spoke only when he was spoken to, and, when he excused himself later, Alice Maynard mumbled something about teaching him a lesson which was totally bewildering to Jennifer.

She did not see Hunter during the rest of the afternoon, but he was leaning against the rails at the far end of the verandah when Mike came to collect her at six that evening. Her heart lurched violently at the sight of him, but Mike had taken her arm and was ushering her towards his sporty Jaguar. She tried to appear indifferent, but, with those hard, accusing eyes following her every step of the way, she felt guilty for no reason at all. Hunter was making her feel like someone going off on a cheap romantic escapade, instead of which she was going to spend the evening with an old and trusted friend who had never so much as touched her hand in anything other than a platonic fashion.

If only she could make Hunter understand how wrong he was, but what would be the use? He believed whatever he pleased, and right this minute he was convinced that she was on her way to a few hours of passion in Mike Hoffman's bed.

CHAPTER SIX

HAVING dinner with Mike Hoffman was the antidote Jennifer had needed desperately. He was someone she could talk to; someone she could confide in. But most of all he was someone she could relax and be herself with. Their relationship with each other had always been comfortable, and without the usual tensions between a man and a woman. Perhaps it was due to the fact that they understood each other so well, she decided as their eyes met across the candlelit table in a quiet corner of the restaurant.

'Are you still cut up over Colin's death?' Mike asked unexpectedly, and the smile left her eyes.

'I shall always regret the fact that such a brilliant surgeon should have lost his life in such a silly accident, but——'

'You're no longer pining for him,' Mike filled in for her when she stopped speaking so abruptly.

'No,' she admitted.

'Has someone else taken his place?'

'No.' It was a deliberate lie, but when she saw the look in his eyes she laughed ruefully and shook her head. 'I never was much good at hiding things from you, was I?'

'It's Hunter Maynard, isn't it.'

It was a statement, not a question, and she looked at him in shocked surprise as she asked, 'What on earth gave you that idea?'

'Men do occasionally have a sixth sense about these things, you know.'

They stared at each other for a time, then she lowered

her glance a little guiltily. 'Mike, I want you to know that I loved and respected Colin very much, and I'm sure we could have made each other very happy.'

'But?' Mike added humorously.

'What I feel for Hunter is totally different.'

'In what way?'

'He attracts me physically in a way no man has ever attracted me before,' she replied with complete honesty. 'It frightens me at times.'

Mike frowned slightly. 'There's nothing wrong with being physically attracted to a man.'

'But it doesn't necessarily mean that you love him, is that what you're saying?' she asked with an embarrassed laugh.

'In a way, yes,' he nodded, then he swallowed down the remainder of his coffee before asking, 'How do you feel about him in other respects?'

Jennifer leaned back in her chair and sighed. 'In these few weeks that I've known him I've been driven to anger more times than I care to mention, and on occasions I've actually been tempted to strike the man!'

'That doesn't sound like you at all,' Mike observed dryly. 'I've always known you as an essentially calm, non-violent sort of girl.'

'I don't quite know myself these days,' she confessed, frowning down at the checkered tablecloth. 'Every time I'm with Hunter he succeeds in shattering my composure, and bringing out the worst in me, but perhaps it's because he makes it so obvious that he despises all women except his mother, of course, and Carla von Brandis.'

'I see,' he smiled faintly, and she felt driven to defend herself.

'I'm not jealous of her, if that's what you're thinking.'

'Aren't you?'

Jennifer smothered her guilt and said instead, 'He's going to marry her.'

'Oh, dear,' he murmured, a peculiar expression on his face as she leaned towards him across the table.

'Mike, he's been hurt before, and I just know that Carla is going to hurt him as well,' she said with some urgency.

A glimmer of surprise lurked in Mike's dark eyes as he observed her closely. 'Are you telling me that, despite the fact that he angers you so much, you can still care what happens to him?'

'I wouldn't like to think of him being hurt again, and . . .' She paused and smiled a sad, twisted little smile. 'I guess I do love him, don't I?'

'I would say you love him too much, but it isn't much use if he has some other girl in his sights,' he put an ungentle finger on an achingly tender spot, and she winced inwardly.

'I know,' she sighed despairingly.

'You said, I believe, that he despises all women,' Mike remarked after a thoughtful silence had elapsed. 'What reason would he have to despise you?'

'He thinks all women are fickle, and he thinks . . .'

'Go on,' Mike prompted abruptly when her voice seemed to grind to a halt.

'He thinks that you and I were lovers once, and that we're picking up our affair where we left off in the past,' she managed after a mental battle with herself. 'He's quite convinced that I'm the kind of girl who hops into bed with every man I meet.'

'The man must be a fool!' Mike exploded angrily, but she shook her head to the contrary, conscious of the curious glances which had been directed at them at the sound of Mike's raised voice.

'He just won't let himself trust a woman again,' she explained quietly.

'Have you made any attempts to alter his opinion of you?'

'I'm afraid not,' she grimaced. 'Every time he accuses me unjustly I become so furious that I play along with him, and let him think the worst.'

'That's not very wise of you, Jennifer,' Mike reprimanded her.

'I know, but——' she gestured helplessly with one slender hand, 'what else can I do, short of having myself medically examined and presenting him with a report to prove that I'm not that sort of girl?' When Mike did not reply, she shrugged and added fatalistically, 'At any rate, there's no point in trying to alter his opinion of my character. He's going to marry Carla, and that's that.'

Mike leaned across the table and covered her hand with his own. 'I wish there was something I could do to help.'

'There's nothing anyone can do,' she replied dully, realising for the first time to what extent she had been defeated by circumstances.

When Mike drove her home later that evening and parked his car in the driveway, Jennifer felt that familiar tension coiling through her, and with it came the suspicion that she was being observed. She was being ridiculous, she told herself, but that gnawing suspicion persisted.

'What I actually wanted to tell you this evening was that I'm returning to Cape Town at the end of this week,' Mike told her when he turned in his seat to face her in the moonlit darkness of his car. 'My stint here in Oudtshoorn is at an end, and I think it's time I started a practice of my own.'

'It's time you found yourself a wife and settled down,' she told him with mock severity.

'When I find the right girl I'll let you know,' he laughed carelessly, and she frowned at him in the darkness.

'I hope you find her soon, and I mean that, Mike.'

His fingers brushed lightly against her lips in a silencing gesture. 'Will you give me a call as soon as you're back in Cape Town?'

'Where will I reach you?'

'I'll be moving into my old flat,' he said, 'and the telephone number is still the same.'

She leaned forward impulsively to kiss him on the cheek. 'I'll give you a call,' she promised. 'And thanks for being such a good listener.'

Moments later she was letting herself into the house with the soft purr of Mike's departing car in her ears. The house was in darkness, but Jennifer made her way up the stairs without difficulty. The light on the top landing had been left on to throw a soft glow over the last flight of steps, but, when she turned off towards her room, a harsh voice made her stop dead in her tracks.

'I take it you had a pleasant evening?'

Determined not to lose her temper with Hunter, she turned slowly to face him as he approached her from the direction of his own bedroom.

'I spent a very pleasant evening, thank you,' she replied with a calm she was far from experiencing as her glance travelled over his tall, disturbingly masculine frame. In a white shirt, unbuttoned almost to his waist, and cream-coloured pants, he looked dangerously tanned and virile, and her senses responded to the magnetism he exuded.

'You'll be seeing each other again soon?' he asked.

'Not for quite a while,' she replied, fighting to control her racing pulse when Hunter finally towered over her. 'Mike is returning to Cape Town at the end of this week.'

'What a pity that your reunion was so brief,' he mocked her, 'but I have no doubt you'll be seeing each other again within a few short weeks.'

There was no point in lying, so she met his gaze unfalteringly, and said lightly, 'We've arranged to meet, yes.'

'That doesn't surprise me,' he smiled derisively, his eyes glittering like cold chips of ice. 'Now that you've managed to get your clutches into him again, you're not going to let go easily, are you?'

Damn the man! she thought. She was doing her level best not to lose her temper with him, while he, on the contrary, appeared to be doing everything within his power to rattle her.

'Please, Mr Maynard,' she managed at last. 'I'm tired, and I don't want to argue with you.'

'I wasn't aware that we were arguing,' he contradicted with raised eyebrows. 'I thought we were discussing the evening you spent with Mike Hoffman.'

'I don't wish to discuss it with you,' she stated bluntly, and his eyebrows rose a fraction higher to form a mocking arch above his eyes.

'Don't tell me you've suddenly developed a sense of shame?'

Forcing down yet another wave of anger, she met his mocking glance unwaveringly, and said with as much calm as she could manage, 'I've never done anything I need be ashamed of, and that's the truth.'

'Do you really expect me to believe you when I know that Mike Hoffman has a reputation for seducing almost every woman he meets?' he demanded, his expression hardening until his features seemed to be carved out of granite.

'Mike has never tried to seduce me, not by word or deed, and he also knows that I would never tolerate it.'

He stared at her in silence for a moment, but she soon realised that she might as well have saved her breath, for his expression remained unaltered.

'I must confess that for a moment I almost believed you, but then experience has taught me that women lie so convincingly.'

'You wouldn't know the truth if it were blazoned in fire before your very eyes,' she retorted sharply, her control slipping dangerously as anger washed over her like a heated wave.

'Perhaps you're right, but I happen to need convincing,' Hunter said harshly, his eyes glittering with a matching anger as he lessened the distance between them, 'and who better than you to do that?'

She should have been prepared for what followed, but her reflexes seemed to have become retarded by the effect of his nearness, and the next instant she found herself crushed against his wide chest with his lips taking possession of hers in a savage kiss that made her senses reel violently. She would have given anything at that moment not to respond, but her body went limp against his as her treacherous emotions soared to unimaginable heights. His hands caressed her freely now, moulding her hips to the thrusting hardness of his before seeking the taut swell of her breasts through the soft silk of her dress. She trembled and raised her hands with the intention of pushing him away, but her fingers somehow became locked behind his dark head where his short, neatly trimmed hair was surprisingly soft to the touch.

No one had ever kissed her like this before, not even Colin, and no man had ever been permitted to touch her with such intimacy, but with Hunter it somehow seemed so right. She loved him. If she had ever doubted it before, then she was certain of it now, but in that moment of mad ecstasy she disregarded the urgent warnings which were flashing through her brain. It was only when Hunter released her as suddenly as he had taken her that she began to realise what a fool she had been.

'Do you usually allow a man such freedom, Sister Casey, or did Mike not satisfy you entirely this evening?'

His words stung deep, branding her a wanton, and before she had time to reconsider, she raised her hand and slapped him a stinging blow across the cheek. The sound seemed to reverberate along the passage, and she was white and trembling with shock when she realised what she had done. Except for the clenching of his hands at his sides, Hunter stood immobile, but as she continued to look up into his eyes she knew the first stirrings of real fear. He was quite capable of retaliating in a similar fashion, she realised that now, but instead he lashed her once more with his tongue.

'The truth hurts, doesn't it?' he remarked cuttingly, then he turned on his heel and walked away, leaving her with the aching knowledge that she had only herself to blame for the conclusions he had reached.

Jennifer was hollow-eyed and pale when she awoke the following morning. She had spent most of the night tossing and turning about in her bed, and it had left her with a feeling of exhaustion she had to cope with for the rest of the day. To avoid Hunter was impossible, but when they did happen to meet he merely treated her with his usual disdain, which was a blessing in some ways, although it hurt in so many others.

She had no idea how she was going to get through the day, let alone the morning, and when Stanley and Carla arrived at Vogelsvlei that afternoon, their cars crunching up the drive with mere seconds in between, Jennifer was beginning to feel like a mechanical robot; doing what she had to do, but doing so without feeling, or enthusiasm.

Tea was served, as usual, on the wide verandah, and the conversation lingered mostly on the latest market price for ostrich feathers, and the best methods in the cultivation of lucerne fields. It was Stanley, however, who finally led the conversation along a totally different avenue.

'They're having the Spring Ball at the Valley Motel this coming Saturday evening,' he announced, manipulating his chair a little closer to Jennifer's. 'Will you go with me, Jennifer?'

She shook her head tiredly. 'I—I don't think——'

'Oh, but you *must* go, Jennifer. It's one of *the* social events of the year,' Alice Maynard remarked, then her searching glance was directed at her son. 'You're going, aren't you, Hunter?'

'I haven't given it much thought,' he shrugged his wide shoulders.

'But you must go, darling,' Carla purred persuasively, her hand caressing his arm. 'You promised you'd take me.'

'I promised nothing of the kind.'

'But you said——'

'I said I would think about it and, quite frankly, I haven't had time to do so,' he interrupted with a harshness Jennifer had not heard him use with Carla before.

'But you'll think about it now, won't you?' Carla persisted in an unperturbed fashion, and when he did not reply at once, she added poutingly, 'Oh, please, Hunter? You know how much I've been looking forward to it.'

Hunter's blue gaze met Jennifer's briefly, but it was as if he were looking right through her without seeing her, then he glanced back at the girl seated beside him, and said irritably, 'Very well, Carla, I'll take you.'

'Hunter!' she cried excitedly, leaning across the arm of her chair to hug him. 'You're so sweet!'

'That's enough of that, my dear Carla,' Hunter reprimanded her with a faintly humorous expression on his chiselled face. 'Now be a good girl and pour me another cup of tea.'

'Anything you say, darling,' Carla replied, jumping obligingly to her feet to do his bidding.

'Hmph!' Alice Maynard grunted disparagingly beneath her breath, but no one seemed to hear her except Jennifer, who smiled inwardly at the older woman's displeasure.

'Would anyone else like a second cup of tea?' Carla queried, adopting the role of hostess easily and gracefully.

Alice and Jennifer both declined, but Stanley said cheerfully, 'I'll have another cup, if you don't mind pouring it, Carla.'

She glanced at Stanley over her shoulder and flashed him a sweet smile. 'Of course I don't mind, silly.'

Jennifer was suddenly alert to something which was happening right before her very eyes. Carla passed Hunter his cup of tea with her usual display of affection, but when she turned to give Stanley his cup, Jennifer could have sworn that a silent message passed between them. She was imagining it, of course, she told herself crossly, and tried to forget it.

She did not imagine, however, the sudden urgency in Stanley's manner when he leaned towards her and asked, 'You will go with me to the Spring Ball, won't you, Jennifer?'

A peculiar silence reigned on Vogelsvlei's verandah. It was almost as if everyone were waiting with some anxiety for her to reply to Stanley's invitation, and moments later she heard herself say, 'I'd like to, and thank you for asking me.'

She felt Hunter's eyes on her, compelling her to look at him, and when she did she felt a strange but powerful tremor rippling through her. He was looking at her with a burning and searching intensity that seemed to probe deep into her soul. Afraid of what he might see, she looked away, and then Carla was saying something which succeeded in recapturing Hunter's attention.

Long after everyone had gone, leaving only Alice and Jennifer on the verandah, she was still suffering from the after-effects of that strange look Hunter had given her. It had left her disturbed and shaken, and feeling very much as if an invisible hand had squeezed her heart until it ached.

'Oh, God!' she thought, passing a tired hand over her eyes. 'Why did I have to love a man like Hunter Maynard?'

If Alice noticed Jennifer's disturbed attitude, then she gave no sign that she did, and merely picked up her crocheting to continue working on it.

Jennifer could not, in all sincerity, say that she looked forward to accompanying Stanley to the Spring Ball at the Valley Motel that Saturday evening, but it was too late now to change her mind. She prepared herself for it with very little enthusiasm, and selected at random a pale blue silk evening gown which was still quite new. Blue was not her favourite colour, but the dress was styled simply, and the material clung softly to the gentle curve of breasts and hips, leaving her smooth shoulders bare except for narrow, corded straps.

She would pass, she decided listlessly, glancing at herself in the mirror. She picked up her brush and pulled it through her naturally wavy hair, but when her hands went up, automatically, to twist it into its usual coil, she decided against it. Just this once she did not care what Hunter thought, and it was, after all, her free evening.

The motel, with its log-cabin appearance, was ablaze with coloured lights when she arrived there with Stanley that evening. The band was blaring out a lively tune while people were trying to make themselves heard above the din, and everyone seemed to know everyone else.

Seated at a table for four behind the large, potted ferns, Jennifer had difficulty in keeping her eyes off Hunter. In a dark, superbly tailored suit, he exuded an aura of virile masculinity which was unmistakable, and her senses stirred sharply each time he passed her chair to take Carla on to the space cleared for dancing. Jennifer had never felt more miserable, and she wished now that she had had the good sense to remain at Vogelsvlei with Alice Maynard. Not once had Hunter asked her to dance; not even on those occasions when Stanley had encouraged Carla on to the floor, and Hunter's lapse had hurt her unbearably.

Jennifer had to admit that Carla, with her dark colouring, looked exquisite in a wine-red evening gown with her liquid brown eyes teasing and enticing whenever they met Hunter's. It was no wonder that Hunter could not keep his eyes off her, and neither, Jennifer noticed, could Stanley. That hungry look was there in his eyes; unveiled, and intense.

There was plenty to eat, but Jennifer had somehow lost her appetite, and neither did she have more to drink than the one glass of wine which Stanley had ordered for her. Stanley, however, seemed to consume a large quantity of alcohol, and Jennifer noticed that she was not the only one who was observing him with a measure of frowning displeasure.

Hunter glared at him from time to time with something close to disgust in his eyes, and Jennifer was fast beginning to experience the same feeling each time she danced with Stanley and had to contend with his whisky breath.

It was well after eleven that evening when a daring young man butted in, and Jennifer was only too relieved to escape from Stanley's arms for a few minutes to bother about protesting.

'My name's Dirk Pienaar,' the young man introduced himself. 'And you're Jennifer Casey.'

'How did you know that?' she asked in surprise.

'We all know about the nursing Sister who's looking after Mrs Maynard until she's well again, and I asked Hunter what your name was.'

'Oh,' she managed, at a loss for words.

'I'm a guide at the Cango Caves,' Dirk Pienaar enlightened her with a flashing smile. 'You must come to the caves before you return to Cape Town and, remember, ask for me.' His smile broadened as he added with some arrogance, 'I'm the best guide they have.'

'I shall remember to ask for you,' she promised with a hint of humour in her voice, and some minutes later he was accompanying her back to her table.

Dirk seemed keen to keep her company when he realised that she would be alone at the table, but she discouraged him, and when he returned to his own table, she slipped outside to enjoy a refreshing stroll in the motel's lush, scented garden.

Keeping to the shadows, Jennifer walked a little distance from the dance hall to escape some of the noise. The grass was soft beneath her feet, muting her footsteps as she approached the two figures standing close together in the darkness beyond a tall shrub. They were totally oblivious of

her approach, and Jennifer, too, was unaware of their presence until the sound of Carla's enraptured voice brought
her to an abrupt halt a little distance from them.

'Oh, Stan, Stan!' Carla was whispering urgently. 'Hold
me! Kiss me, please!'

Stanley's soft, intoxicated laugh reached Jennifer's
shocked ears, and he followed it up by murmuring huskily,
'You're a little devil, Carla, my love.'

Jennifer shrank farther into the shadows as she witnessed
the two figures melting into one. Afraid to move, and sick
with disgust, she remained where she was for a moment
longer. They had planned this, Jennifer knew it now. They
had known that during the course of the evening they would
have the opportunity to be alone together, and Hunter had
obviously given them that opportunity, although unsuspectingly. Jennifer came to her senses as Hunter's image
leapt into her mind, and it was the thought of him that made
her retrace her steps as quickly, and as silently as she could
manage in her distressed state.

To her horror, Hunter was the first person she met when
she reached the terrace. In her haste she collided with him
in the shadows, and she was pale and shaken when he stead-
ied her on her feet.

'Have you seen Carla?' he asked abruptly, looking at a
point somewhere beyond her creamy shoulder.

'Well, I—no, I'm afraid I haven't,' she lied desperately,
hating Carla for what she was obviously doing to Hunter.

'I shall have to look for her, then,' he announced, and she
went cold with fright when she thought of him striding
unsuspectingly in the direction of the garden where Carla
and Stanley could possibly still be locked in each other's
arms.

'Hunter . . .' The use of his name was unintentional, but

it stopped him in his stride, and when he turned slowly to face her, her frantic mind could think of only one possible way to prevent him from walking in on that little scene she had witnessed moments ago. 'I know it's late, and almost time to return home,' she smiled up at him shakily, and, she hoped, persuasively. 'But you owe me a dance, I think.'

His eyebrows rose mockingly. 'It's customary for the man to ask the woman, not vice versa.'

'I know,' she said, her cheeks burning. She hated herself for being so brazen, but she had started something which she had to finish. 'Are you going to refuse me?'

For a moment it seemed as if he were going to do exactly that, then he smiled twistedly. 'Never let it be said that I refused a woman something she wanted badly enough to ask for.'

The sardonic gleam in his eyes told her exactly what he was thinking when he led her on to the dance floor, but she would rather have him think the worst of her, than to be disillusioned by the one girl he seemed to trust.

Questions for which she could find no answers ricocheted through her mind, but not for long. Hunter's hand was firm and warm against the hollow of her back while they danced in perfect unison to the dreamy beat of the music. No girl in her right mind could be this close to Hunter without being aware of him as a man, and Jennifer was no exception. Carla and Stanley no longer claimed priority in her thoughts when Hunter drew her closer until their bodies became fused together. She could not think, anyway, with several volts of electricity charging through her. His thighs brushed against hers, while his masculine cologne stirred her senses, and his nearness was suddenly more intoxicating than several glasses of wine could ever have been.

This was crazy! Jennifer told herself, but she definitely

felt lightheaded, and the sensual touch of his hand against her back did not improve matters as he guided her steps expertly and silently across the crowded floor.

She found herself wishing that this moment would go on for ever, but the music ended abruptly, and just as abruptly Hunter released her. His hooded glance met hers, but only briefly, then he took her arm and guided her back to their table.

To Jennifer's relief they found Carla and Stanley waiting for them, and no one, not even Jennifer, would have guessed that anything had happened between them if she had not witnessed it with her own eyes some minutes ago. It sickened her, this deceit, and she had lost a great deal of her respect for Stanley, as well as for Carla, in the process.

'Come on, Carla,' Hunter said abruptly. 'It's time I took you home.'

'Oh, but darling,' Carla pouted with an injured look on her lovely face, 'you're surely going to have one more dance with me before we go?'

'You've missed out, my dear,' Hunter remarked dryly as he picked up her wrap and draped it about her shoulders. 'I've already had the last dance for the evening, and now it's time to go home.'

His tone of voice did not encourage an argument, and Carla relented with a surprising meekness to his demands.

'I think I'd like to go home as well, Stanley,' Jennifer said quickly, picking up her own wrap and evening purse.

'Sure,' Stanley nodded, and Jennifer was mildly surprised to see that he was still steady on his feet as they followed Hunter and Carla from the building to where their cars were parked.

They were some distance out of town when Stanley glanced at Jennifer and said casually, 'You're very quiet.'

'I'm troubled,' she confessed and, turning slightly in her seat to face him, she said accusingly, 'I happened to see you with Carla in the garden this evening.'

'Oh,' he said, looking decidedly uncomfortable as he stared straight ahead of him to where the twin beams of the car sliced through the darkness. 'I can explain, Jennifer.'

'I wish you would,' she replied crossly.

'Carla's really the biggest flirt there is, and it's very difficult for a man to resist her, you know.'

Jennifer's faintly cynical smile went unnoticed. 'It didn't seem to me as if you were trying very hard to resist her advances. It seemed, in fact, as if you were offering as much encouragement as you were receiving.'

'You're mistaken, Jennifer,' he argued with a laugh that sounded forced. 'I can only plead that I was a little light-headed.'

'You're admitting, then, that you had too much to drink this evening?'

'Yes, Sister Casey, I'm admitting it,' he replied unashamedly, and drove on in silence for quite some time before he said hesitantly, 'You won't tell Hunter about—about what you saw, will you?'

His weakness had invited her sympathy before, but now she despised him for it as she said stiffly, 'He wouldn't believe me even if I did.'

'You're right, he wouldn't,' Stanley laughed, sounding a little more confident, and he did not speak again until he had parked his car in front of Vogelsvlei's homestead. 'Are you angry with me, Jennifer?' he asked now, his hand on her arm preventing her from getting out of the car.

'Disappointed is the word,' she said coldly. 'I'd credited you with more sense.'

'I'm sorry.'

'So am I.'

Twisting her arm free of his clasp, she wished him a cool 'goodnight' and, slipping out of his car, she hurried up the steps to the front door.

Despite the late hour, Jennifer could not fall asleep that night. She tossed about restlessly in her bed until long after she had heard Hunter enter the house, and she finally decided to seek a little fresh air in the hope of clearing her mind of the thoughts that churned through it.

The night air was cool against her flushed face when she stepped out on to the balcony, and her fingers automatically tightened the belt of her silk robe about her slim waist. The moon was full in the star-clustered sky, but it was Carla and Stanley who occupied her thoughts at that moment, and not the enchantment of the moonlit night.

If only she could know what they were up to, then she might find some way of warning Hunter. *If only*—what futile words! Hunter would never believe her, and in the end her intentions would be misconstrued. He was indeed a fool to put his trust in Carla if she could deceive him with so little effort, but there was nothing Jennifer could do about it, and he would, in the end, be hurt once again.

Something, a sound perhaps, made her realise that she was no longer alone, and she turned warily to see Hunter, still fully clothed except for his jacket, walking towards her in the moonlit darkness of the balcony.

'It appears we both have the same problem,' he remarked mockingly when he reached her side. 'Couldn't you sleep?'

'No,' she replied, conscious of being dressed only in her night attire with a thin robe as protection, and of the uneven beat of her treacherous heart.

'One way and another this evening wasn't quite a success, was it.'

'No.'

'Were you hoping that I'd take your flirtation seriously?'

'No!' she cried fiercely, grateful that he could not see the flush of embarrassment staining her cheeks.

'I don't particularly care for one-sided conversations,' he remarked caustically.

'I'm sorry,' she whispered and, unable to bear his disturbing nearness a moment longer, she turned and fled towards her room.

'Jenny!'

His voice stopped her on the threshold, and she turned to see him approach her slowly, his tall frame silhouetted against the velvety night sky. No one, since her father's death, had ever called her 'Jenny' and, coming from Hunter, who had never addressed her in any other form but 'Sister Casey', it sounded odd, yet somehow pleasing.

He was standing directly in front of her now, the masculine scent of his body filling her nostrils and stirring her senses madly as he raised a hand to finger the silken strands of her honey-gold hair which was hanging loose and rather untidily about her shoulders. For one who had insisted that she kept her hair tied up in a rigid knot on her head, he seemed to be finding enjoyment in running his strong fingers through it.

Jennifer's heart was beating so fast now that she could hardly breathe when she felt the sensual pressure of his fingers against the nape of her neck. His breath mingled with hers as he murmured her name once more, then his mouth found hers with a potent sensuality that parted her lips and drove every scrap of rational thought from her mind. His free arm was about her waist, moulding her soft contours to the hard length of his body, and she felt again that electrifying current of turbulent emotions surging through her.

'This is wrong,' the voice of her conscience warned, but his hand had slipped inside the opening of her silk robe to seek the soft swell of her breast beneath the lace of her nightgown, and the voice of her conscience was abruptly silenced by the pleasurable sensations rippling through her receptive body.

She was only vaguely conscious now of being urged backwards into her room, and it was only when she felt herself going down on to her bed, with Hunter on top of her, that she started to protest. His lips, however, trailed a path of destruction across one smooth shoulder down to her breast which had been exposed by his impatient, probing hand, and quite suddenly all desire to resist deserted her.

'Hunter!' she breathed his name ecstatically, no longer conscious of what she was doing as she wrapped her eager arms about his strong neck and clung to him rapturously.

His tantalising, feather-light caresses awakened her to a new urgency spiralling through her heated body; an urgency and a need which was rising swiftly to match his, but when she felt his hand sliding possessively up along her smooth, naked thigh, she came to her senses with a violent start.

'Don't!' she begged huskily, struggling beneath him now. 'Please, don't!'

Hunter drew away from her slightly, but he did not release her entirely. She could not read the expression in his shadowed face above her own, but when he spoke the mockery in his voice sliced through her like a heated blade.

'You play the part of the frightened virgin to perfection.

Others may believe you, but you don't really fool me.'

Her hand rose involuntarily to strike him, but hard fingers fastened on to her slender wrist, and the pressure they exerted made her cry out in pain.

'You lifted your hand to me once before,' he said gratingly, 'but this time you're going to pay for trying to repeat the performance.'

His hard mouth came down on to hers in a savage kiss that bruised her soft lips, and brought tears to her eyes, but his actions didn't stop there. His hands were insistent as they roamed over her body, and she felt they insulted her in the most humiliating way. She tried to cry out, to beg for mercy, but, with his mouth against hers, her cry was nothing but a low groan deep down in her aching throat. She fought him off with every particle of strength she possessed, but her treacherous body finally responded to the violation of his hands, and he did not cease his intimate caresses until she found herself trembling on the brink of a desire that filled her with the aching, and alien, need for fulfilment.

Her hands moved of their own volition to seek the smooth, hard flesh of his muscled shoulders beneath his shirt, and her body arched towards his in abject surrender. She had gone beyond the point of caring, knowing for the first time in her life the desire to be possessed by a man, but Hunter had achieved what he had set out to accomplish and, thrusting her from him, he rose to his feet to tower over her in the darkness.

'Goodnight, Sister Casey,' he said with a savage mockery in his voice that made her flinch visibly. 'I hope you sleep well.'

He was gone before she could reply, leaving her shaking uncontrollably from head to foot as if with the fever. She was, at first, bewildered and confused by what had occurred, but when her emotions plummeted sickeningly, she wept tears of humiliation and despair. She felt degraded and cheap, and she hated him for doing this to her, but she hated herself more for being so weak.

CHAPTER SEVEN

THEY left Vogelsvlei early on the Monday morning and headed towards Port Elizabeth where Alice Maynard was to see the specialist Dr Tremayne had called in to her initially. As before, Jennifer sat in front with Hunter, leaving Alice to herself on the back seat, but on this occasion Jennifer felt more than just slightly uncomfortable. She had lived through an awkward Sunday during which she had tried unsuccessfully to stay out of Hunter's way, and even now she still squirmed inwardly at the memory of the passion he had aroused with such ease within her.

Jennifer spoke very little throughout the journey. It took them several hours, and she was relieved when at last they booked into an expensive-looking hotel on the Port Elizabeth beach-front. Jennifer and Alice were both given rooms on the third floor, while Hunter was shown to a room on the fourth, but there was very little time to look around and, after a quick lunch, Jennifer accompanied Hunter and his mother to the Medical Centre in the heart of the city.

Alice Maynard was nervous, Jennifer could tell this by the way she moved jerkily on her crutches when the receptionist accompanied her into the examination room, and some of her nervousness transferred itself to Jennifer, who sat stiffly in her chair in the spacious waiting-room. Hunter sat facing her, but he had buried himself behind a magazine, and it was only when he lit a cigarette that she realised he was just as anxious as she.

The examination had lasted not more than a half hour,

but to Jennifer it had felt like hours, and Alice Maynard's exhausted appearance indicated that it had felt the same to her. They glanced at her questioningly, but she gestured them to silence, and it was a sombre trio who drove away from the Medical Centre minutes later.

'It's nothing serious,' Alice assured Jennifer when she glimpsed the anxiety in her eyes. 'I'm merely too tired to talk.'

Jennifer sighed inwardly with relief, and settled down in her seat. It was only when they reached the hotel and had ushered Alice up to her room that they questioned her in earnest.

'What's the verdict?' Hunter asked now, his voice abrupt, and some of his anxiety still clearly visible in the taut line of his hard jaw.

Alice Maynard leaned back in her easy chair and closed her eyes. 'A full report will be sent to Dr Tremayne, but the specialist considers me well enough to try using walking sticks in future instead of these cumbersome crutches.' She opened her eyes suddenly and smiled up at them. 'He said that my hip has healed perfectly, but that I still had to take care.'

'That means that I shall have to think of returning to Cape Town,' Jennifer smiled down at her, but the smile was not echoed in her heart.

'Not yet, Jennifer,' Alice protested at once. 'I don't think I'm ready yet to do without your assistance.'

'Of course you are,' Jennifer contradicted gently. 'You hardly need my assistance at the moment as it is.'

'And who, do you think, will help me with my exercises?'

'You no longer need those vigorous exercises, Mrs Maynard, and you know that,' Jennifer reminded her.

'Don't argue with me, Jennifer,' Alice complained. 'I'm

tired, and I think I'll have dinner sent up to my room this evening.'

Jennifer nodded. 'That's a good idea.'

'Why don't you take Jennifer to dinner this evening, Hunter?' Alice surprised Jennifer with her suggestion to her son. 'The hotel has an excellent night-club, and there's usually a dance band playing for those who want to dance.'

'Mrs Maynard, please!' Jennifer begged, flushing with embarrassment and not daring to glance in Hunter's direction. 'I'm perfectly capable of amusing myself for the evening, and there's no need for——'

'I'd be delighted if you would have dinner with me,' Hunter remarked quietly, surprising Jennifer still further.

'There, you see?' Alice exclaimed triumphantly, but when Jennifer continued to hesitate, she added persuasively, 'It would please me very much if you would accept Hunter's invitation.'

Jennifer could not look at the man standing so motionless beside her. She felt as if she had been driven into a corner and, sighing inwardly, she relented. 'Very well, Mrs Maynard, you win.'

'Good,' Alice smiled delightedly. 'Now go, please, and leave me to get some rest.'

When Jennifer stood facing Hunter outside Alice's door moments later, she was forced to meet his glance, but his face was expressionless, and those narrowed eyes shuttered.

'I'll make the necessary arrangements, and meet you here within an hour,' he said in a clipped voice, then he turned on his heel and strode towards the lift.

Jennifer could think of nothing she wanted less than having to spend an evening in Hunter's company. The mere thought of it terrified her, and her stomach felt as if it had been twisted into a painful knot when it was eventually time for her to go out and meet him. She took one last look at herself in the mirror to satisfy herself that she was dressed suitably for the occasion, and she was trying desperately to control the trembling of her limbs when she stepped out into the passage to find Hunter waiting for her.

His wide-shouldered appearance in his dark, impeccably tailored evening suit had a devastating effect on her nervous system, but it was the brooding intensity of his eyes that had such an odd effect on her breathing. His glance travelled slowly and systematically down the length of her, taking in the emerald green silk of her dress, and leaving her with the alarming feeling that he had stripped her down to her skin. It was a shattering experience, and it left her feeling heated and flustered. His lips twitched, as if he was fully aware of her discomfort, then his hand was beneath her elbow, and he was guiding her towards the lift.

In the close confines of the lift cage which was bearing them upwards to the night-club on the tenth floor, Jennifer studied Hunter unobtrusively. There was something different about him this evening; a subtle sensuality of movement perhaps, and it disturbed her intensely, making her aware of her femininity in a way he had never done before.

She wished he would say something; *anything* to relieve the tense silence between them, but the doors of the lift slid open at that moment, and some of the tension eased. A red-coated steward ushered them to a table in the already crowded room, and Hunter ordered a bottle of wine to be brought to their table while they waited for the meal he had ordered.

Facing each other across the candlelit table, they discussed his mother's progress in detail while they sipped their wine. It was a safe topic, but when their meal was eventually placed before them the conversation took a turn towards the personal.

'You seemed rather reluctant to dine with me this evening,' he remarked mockingly. 'Did you plan to spend your evening with someone else, perhaps?'

'Don't be silly,' she said, still fighting down her nervousness. 'I don't know anyone here in Port Elizabeth.'

'I was merely speculating,' he observed dryly, but she sensed that he did not quite believe her.

'If you must know, I was reluctant to accept your invitation because I felt that your mother had forced your hand.'

'I'd like to set your mind at rest on that score,' he replied, his compelling gaze meeting hers. 'I had my invitation ready, but my mother merely beat me to it.'

Jennifer observed him through lowered lashes. 'I don't think I can believe that.'

'Please yourself,' he shrugged, his mouth tightening.

'Now I've annoyed you.'

'I've never met a more annoying woman in my life, but I dare say I'll survive the evening,' he remarked caustically.

'Mr Maynard, I——'

'Hunter,' he interrupted, his eyes glittering strangely as they met hers. 'I thought we'd dispensed with formalities the other evening.'

'I don't——' she began in something close to anger, then she faltered, blushed, and swallowed nervously.

'You were going to say?'

'I can't remember,' she shook her head, lowering her eyes to her plate. 'I don't suppose it was important.'

'I don't suppose it was,' he mocked her faintly, and when

she looked up at him suspiciously, he leaned towards her across the table and said: 'You have lovely eyes, Jenny, but I wonder sometimes what lies hidden beneath those cool depths.'

'Why do you call me Jenny?' she asked, slanting a curious glance at him.

'I like the sound of it.' A faint smile touched his usually stern mouth. 'Do you mind?'

She shook her head and swallowed down the lump which had risen unexpectedly to her throat. 'The only one who ever called me Jenny was my father.'

A gleam of mockery lit his eyes. 'I hope you don't think of me as your father.'

'That was the farthest thought from my mind,' she assured him stiffly. 'You're not at all what I would call a father image.'

'Do I sense a veiled insult there somewhere?'

'What I said was not meant as an insult.'

He held her glance effortlessly for a moment before he concentrated once more on his food, and Jennifer followed his example without much enthusiasm.

'Tell me about your family,' he said at length, and Jennifer glanced up at him with a measure of surprise in her wide hazel eyes.

'My parents died some years ago, but I have a sister who lives in Johannesburg.'

His eyebrows rose mockingly. 'Is that all there is to tell?'

Jennifer stared down at her plate and frowned. 'My family history is about as uninteresting as this leatherised piece of steak.'

'Shall I order something else for you?' Hunter asked at once, but she shook her head hastily.

'I'm not very hungry.'

'Neither am I,' he admitted just as the band resumed its playing and, holding out his hand towards her, he asked, 'Shall we dance instead?'

She was tempted to refuse, but she could not ignore the challenge in his eyes as they met hers and, praying that her nervousness would not show, she placed her hand in his.

Hunter held her close, too close, as he guided her expertly among several other couples who had ventured on to the floor. Their bodies touched, and an awareness sparked between them as it had never done before. She tried to draw away, but his arm tightened about her waist, and the spark became a flame, melting her rigidity until she relaxed against him to enjoy this brief moment of closeness they shared. There would not be another moment like this for her; she dared not allow it, and neither would she encourage it.

Hunter's nearness was a bitter-sweet agony that brought back memories of the Spring Ball two nights ago, and the one dance they had shared because she had been afraid that he might find Carla and Stanley embracing in the garden. What had happened that night after the dance was something she dared not think about, but she was incapable of curbing her thoughts, and her mind conjured up every single incident until her skin tingled with the memory of his touch. Her pulse quickened and, angry with herself, she faltered.

'Is something wrong?' Hunter asked at once, and she raised her glance no higher than his hard jaw.

'I think I'd like to return to our table, if you don't mind.'

She was relieved that he did not question her further, but merely slipped his hand beneath her elbow to guide her back to their table, and to the meal they had left practically untouched. He picked up the bottle of wine and filled up their glasses, but as they raised them to their lips, their eyes met and held. Jennifer experienced an odd feeling of suspension and, holding her breath, she sustained his probing glance as if it were the lifeline which would prevent her from falling. His eyes flickered strangely, and his chiselled mouth curved in that faint suggestion of a smile, then his glance travelled down to where her pulse was beating erratically at the base of her throat, and lower still to where her small breasts were now straining against the silk of her dress.

A wave of heat surged into her cheeks, and she took a quick sip of wine to steady herself, but her hand was shaking to such an extent that she almost spilled some of the liquid on to the tablecloth. '*Damn* Hunter!' she thought angrily and, keeping her gaze averted, she tried to regain what was left of her composure. It was not new to her, this power he had to disturb her usually calm disposition, but she dared not let him know what a fool she had been to lay her heart at his feet.

The lights were dimmed, an indication that the floor show was about to begin and, moments later, a curvaceous young woman was caught in the spotlight as she stepped on to the low platform. The band leader called her 'Louella', and then the introduction was played to the song she was to sing. Her voice, Jennifer discovered, had an attractive, husky quality to it which was suited to the words of the song. It lured and enticed, and Jennifer felt certain that there was not a man in that room who did not feel that the song had been intended for him alone. Jennifer glanced covertly at Hunter, but his face remained impassive, so she returned her attention to the girl who had dislodged the microphone from its stand to move in and out among the tables. Her dress was of a shimmering gold material which was slit up the sides to expose shapely thighs, and it was cut daringly low at the neckline to reveal the curve of her breasts.

Jennifer could hardly restrain her surprise when the singer paused beside their table some moments later. With her blonde hair falling in a seductive veil across her face, Louella sang her song for Hunter alone. Jennifer held her breath, but Hunter did not bat an eyelid as the girl slid a caressing hand along his arm to his shoulder, and her voice became throatier as she leaned towards him with an alluring smile on her lips, giving him an unstinted view of her bulging breasts. Hunter did not waste the opportunity either, Jennifer noticed, but, unlike the others, he did not place his hand on her curvaceous hips in an effort to entice her on to his lap. He appeared to be totally unmoved by the little act which was being played out solely for him, and neither did he display the slightest sign of emotion when Louella perched herself brazenly on his knee to run her fingers through his crisp dark hair.

More than a little horrified, Jennifer observed this embarrassing display intently, and it was at this point that Hunter's glance met hers. There was no time to conceal her disgust, and the mocking light in his eyes told her that he had glimpsed it, but suddenly she did not care. He could know exactly what she thought of the entire distasteful incident.

Louella slid off his lap and moved on with obvious reluctance to a table a little distance from theirs, but she did not repeat her performance, and her eyes darted back continuously to Hunter's broad-shouldered, imposing frame. Slowly, her hips swaying in time to the beat of the music, she made her way back to the platform, and when the song finally ended she opened her arms wide to receive the applause which was enthusiastic and prolonged.

The lights came on once more, and that, Jennifer hoped, would be the last they would see of the seductive Louella, but she was mistaken. That curvaceous body in the revealing, shimmering dress was making its way towards their table, and Jennifer stiffened automatically.

'Hello, Hunter,' the girl said with unbelievable familiarity, her silvery blonde hair swinging freely about her naked shoulders, and Jennifer almost choked on her surprise. 'I never imagined I'd see you here of all places. What brings you to Port Elizabeth?'

'My mother had to see a specialist,' Hunter explained briefly, pulling up a chair for her and seeing her seated.

'Oh, yes, I'd heard about the nasty fall she'd had,' Louella replied vaguely, then those heavily made up eyes studied Jennifer with a speculative gleam in their cool depths before focussing on Hunter once more. 'You're a sly one, I must say. The last time I saw you, you had that dark-haired little Carla spitting fire darts at us, but here I find you with someone else altogether.'

Hunter made the introductions in his usual formal manner and explained, 'Jennifer is taking care of my mother.'

Louella promptly lost interest in Jennifer, but Jennifer felt embarrassingly conspicuous with almost the entire room's attention being focussed on them. After all, the singer's anatomy was of the kind most men would admire when they thought their wives were not looking.

'Hunter, darling,' that husky voice was purring, 'when I was booked to sing at one of your Oudtshoorn hotels, I thought I was going to be bored to tears until I met you, but I never imagined we would meet again, and most certainly not here in Port Elizabeth.' A manicured hand sought his across the table. 'How long are you staying?'

'We leave for Oudtshoorn tomorrow morning.'

'How fortuitous!' Louella exclaimed delightedly. 'I have to be in Plettenberg Bay tomorrow evening. Do you think you could give me a lift?'

Jennifer held her breath, but Hunter glanced beyond the girl and back. 'I think the band leader is trying to catch your eye, Louella.'

'I sing my last number at eleven-thirty,' the girl said, rising from her chair and not pursuing the subject of the lift, but her smile was inviting as she added: 'If you've nothing better to do round about the time I finish here, come up to my room and we'll have a party for two.'

Jennifer had never felt more like an unwanted third and, without so much as a glance in her direction, Louella returned to the platform to proceed with her next number.

'Come on,' Hunter said abruptly, and when Jennifer's questioning glance met his, he said: 'We're going for a drive.'

She could feel the anger in his touch as he placed her silk wrap about her shoulders, but she did not question it. She knew the reason, she told herself, and jealousy such as she had never known before shot like a searing flame through her. He wanted to be with Louella, but instead he was saddled with someone he had never particularly liked.

The air was cool and fresh outside, and Hunter did not drive far before parking his Mercedes in the well-lit street, then he turned towards her abruptly and asked, 'Do you feel like stretching your legs?'

Jennifer nodded and climbed out of the car to feel the tangy air of the sea against her face. If she closed her eyes she could almost believe she was in Cape Town, she thought as Hunter took her arm and led her across the busy street.

'Where are we going?' she asked curiously.

'I believe there's an interesting walk through Happy

Valley.' He glanced at her briefly and mockingly. 'Feel like risking it with me?'

'I could do with some fresh air and exercise,' she replied with forced casualness, looking ahead of her to where the coloured lights marked out the winding paths among the trees and shrubs.

They were not the only people to enjoy this picturesque walk, but Jennifer kept a safe distance between Hunter and herself as they strolled past lily ponds and miniature waterfalls. They walked in silence, but she was aware of him with every fibre of her being, and her nerves vibrated each time his arm brushed against hers accidentally.

They crossed a small wooden bridge and strolled into the deepening shadows beyond it, but her heart almost leapt out of her breast when she felt his hand gripping her waist while he edged her farther into the shadows with his body. She guessed his intentions, and although every part of her yearned for his lips and his arms, she twisted herself free and placed a safe distance between them once again.

'If you don't mind I'd prefer to keep on walking,' she said quickly when she sensed that he was about to reach for her again, and as her eyes became accustomed to the darkness she saw his arms drop to his sides.

'What are you afraid of, Jenny?' he mocked her. 'Me . . . or yourself?'

She still felt raw inside at the memory of the humiliation she had suffered at his hands barely two nights ago, and she said tritely, 'I didn't come here with you to be mauled.'

The electrifying silence was disturbed only by the faint sound of the surf, then Hunter asked harshly, 'Why did you come with me, then? Did you think I'd be content to walk next to you all the way without attempting to touch you?'

She was angry now; angry with herself because of the

longing within her which she could not suppress entirely, and angry with Hunter for imagining she would fall into his arms at the drop of a hat, and when she finally spoke her voice was bitingly cold.

'If you're in need of physical excitement, Hunter, then I suggest you accept Louella's invitation.'

'You know, that's what I like about women like Louella,' he told her gratingly after another frightening silence had prevailed. 'They don't pretend to be what they're not.'

'Then you're welcome to her.'

'Thank you,' he said crushingly. 'I was hoping you would say that.'

His fingers bit into the soft flesh of her arm, and she was practically dragged all the way back to where he had parked his car. He was furious, she knew that, but she could not understand why. If he had wanted to be with Louella he had only needed to say so without creating that unpleasant scene. Why he should be angry now that his plan had succeeded, she had no idea, but then, she supposed, she would never understand Hunter entirely. It pleased him, perhaps, to hurt her, and if that had been his objective, then he had succeeded admirably.

When they reached the hotel Hunter said an abrupt 'Goodnight' to her in the foyer, and she was left to make her own way up to the third floor in the lift. In the privacy of her room she tried to ease the tension from her body, but it returned the moment her glance fell on her travelling clock which she had placed on the bedside cupboard.

Eleven-thirty! Louella had said that she sang her last number at eleven-thirty, and they had returned just in time for Hunter to join her for the intimate little party in her bedroom.

'Oh, God!' Jennifer groaned as she fell across the bed and

buried her face in the pillows. Nothing made sense any more. Carla had made it quite clear that she was going to marry Hunter, yet at the first available opportunity she was languishing in Stanley's arms. Hunter, it seemed, was not particular in whose arms he found himself, and heaven only knew what kind of loyalty he and Carla had sworn to. One thing was clear, however. He might despise all women, but he obviously could not do without them.

Jennifer tried to banish all thoughts from her mind while she undressed herself and climbed into bed, but one thought persisted maddeningly. Hunter was probably with the seductive Louella right that minute, and Jennifer could not bear the painful images that flashed through her tortured mind; images of Hunter and Louella, and a passion shared.

He was always condemning her unjustly for supposedly lacking in morals, but where was the morality in what he was doing at that moment?

'Dear God!' Jennifer groaned into the darkness. 'Losing Colin was nothing like this. Help me! Help me, *please*!'

She had no idea what time it was when she finally managed to fall asleep, but she awoke the following morning with a throbbing headache. She was served breakfast in her room, but she couldn't face anything except a strong cup of coffee, and she popped a couple of aspirins into her mouth to swallow them down with the first mouthful.

Hunter had said that he wanted to leave no later than eight that morning and, glancing at her travelling clock, she hastily packed her suitcase before going along to Alice Maynard's room.

Alice was stomping about the room on her crutches when Jennifer entered and placed her suitcase against the wall close to the door. The older woman's tight-lipped expression reminded Jennifer very much of Hunter at that moment and, crossing the room towards her, she asked tentatively, 'Is something the matter, Mrs Maynard?'

'I'm furious, that's what!' Alice exploded, thumping a crutch against the carpeted floor very much as one would stamp one's foot. 'Hunter has just been in to tell me he's giving some girl called Louella a lift to Plettenberg Bay!'

Jennifer tried to ignore the pain that seemed to tear at her insides, and said with her usual calm, 'What's so terrible about that?'

'You know what a stink he was in to get back to the farm, and now there's suddenly time to stay over for the night at the hotel in Plettenberg Bay where this girl has supposedly been booked to sing.' She scowled angrily. 'I smell a rat, I tell you, and that rat is called Louella!'

Jennifer went cold, but her face mirrored no expression as she glanced at the woman before her. 'Shall I call a porter to collect our suitcases?'

'Yes!' Alice Maynard barked at her, but a rueful expression flitted across her face the next instant. 'I'm sorry, Jennifer. I shouldn't be snapping at you.'

'I understand.'

Grey eyes regarded Jennifer thoughtfully for a moment, then she said with a curious intonation in her voice, 'Do you, I wonder?'

A puzzled frown creased Jennifer's brow, but she had long since discovered that it was futile trying to analyse Alice Maynard and her son, and it was with this thought in mind that she crossed the room towards the telephone to request a porter to come up and collect their suitcases.

Hunter's silver Mercedes was parked at the entrance to the hotel, and fifteen minutes later they were seated in the back, waiting for Louella to put in an appearance. Another fifteen minutes passed, and Hunter, leaning against the side of the car with his arms folded across his chest, muttered something uncomplimentary about women never being on time.

This was just too much for Alice Maynard and, putting her head out of the window, she said icily, 'I beg your pardon, Hunter. We were here well before the time you said you wanted to leave.'

'I wasn't referring to you, Mother,' he replied angrily, sliding behind the wheel and agitatedly lighting a cigarette.

'May I suggest, then, that you refer your insults to the woman who's caused this delay, and not to women in general?'

'For God's sake, Mother, get off my back!' Hunter exploded harshly, making Jennifer jump, but his mother was unperturbed by his display of anger.

'You're a fool, Hunter, and I shan't waste my sympathy on you if you don't come to your senses in a hurry.'

Hunter turned in his seat to frown at his mother. 'I don't need your sympathy, merely your silence.'

His eyes flashed a warning, but Alice Maynard refused to heed it as her own anger rose sharply. 'Why should I sit back silently and meekly while my son seems to be determined to ruin his future?'

'I know what I'm doing, Mother.'

'I'm beginning to doubt it, but don't say I didn't warn you,' Alice remarked coldly.

During the tense silence that followed Jennifer found herself wondering confusedly at the reason behind this verbal altercation between mother and son, but she was still confused moments later when Hunter crushed his cigarette into the ashtray.

'There's Louella,' he muttered and, leaving them alone in the car, he went forward to meet the girl who was pushing her way through the swinging glass doors at that moment.

Two porters, each carrying at least three suitcases, followed close on her heels, but it was not the porters nor the amount of luggage that drew their attention. It was Louella's tight-fitting slacks and skimpy sweater that made both Jennifer as well as Alice Maynard draw in their breaths sharply. They did not need X-ray vision to see that Louella had nothing on beneath her sweater, while the low-cut neckline left nothing to the imagination, but in the daylight Jennifer did notice that Louella's blonde hair had been artificially acquired.

'Heaven help us!' Alice exclaimed in a shocked voice. 'Will you look at that?'

Jennifer turned instead from the sight of the woman approaching the car on Hunter's arm, and only one glance at Alice's face was enough to make her say anxiously, 'You're upsetting yourself, Mrs Maynard, and I can't allow that.'

'Can you blame me?' Alice demanded on a slightly hysterical note. 'For Hunter's sake I was prepared to tolerate Carla, but can you imagine what would happen if he should bring that creature to Vogelsvlei?'

'Please, Mrs Maynard,' Jennifer said sternly, thrusting aside her own concern. 'If you don't stop this I shall have to give you a sedative.'

Alice closed her eyes for a moment, but when she opened them again moments later she was perfectly controlled. 'I'll behave.'

A wave of exotic perfume accompanied Louella into the car, and Hunter introduced her briefly to his mother before returning to the near impossible task of finding room for her suitcases in the boot of the Mercedes. When at last he slid behind the wheel and started the car, his face was an expressionless mask, but Jennifer somehow sensed his irritation, and she had difficulty in suppressing the smile which threatened to lift the corners of her generous mouth.

'It was wonderful of you to offer me this lift, Hunter,' Louella was saying, her husky voice coated with honey, and her suffocating perfume cloying the interior of the car. 'I simply dreaded having to take the bus. It's such a long and tiring journey.'

'It's my pleasure, Louella.'

'Hmph!' Alice grunted disdainfully, but the traffic was heavy, and the sound went unnoticed.

CHAPTER EIGHT

LOUELLA somehow dominated the conversation all the way from Port Elizabeth to Plettenberg Bay, and her husky voice, like her perfume, became a permanent fixture in the car. Once, when Jennifer's eyes met Hunter's in the rear view mirror, she was almost certain that she glimpsed a look of angry exasperation there, but she could have imagined it, she told herself afterwards, for in no other way did he give any indication that he did not enjoy Louella's company.

They arrived at Plettenberg Bay in time for lunch, and afterwards Jennifer accompanied Alice Maynard up to her room, leaving Hunter in the hotel dining-room with Louella.

'I just couldn't stand that woman's voice a moment longer,' Alice complained loudly in the lift that took them up to the sixth floor, and Jennifer agreed with her in silence.

Restlessness drove Jennifer from her own room later that afternoon. A stroll on the beach would perhaps blow some of the cobwebs from her mind, she decided when she crossed the spacious, luxuriously carpeted foyer of the hotel.

'Well, this must be my lucky day!' a young man exclaimed, falling into step beside her, and when she glanced at him blankly, he said: 'Don't you remember me, Sister Casey?'

His face seemed vaguely familiar, she realised as they walked out on to the patio and headed towards the steps leading down to the beach. 'I know we've met before, but I——'

'Dirk Pienaar,' he refreshed her memory at once. 'We met at the Spring Ball at the Valley Motel, remember?'

'Oh, yes, you're a guide at the Cango Caves,' she recalled now, taking in his dark hair which was cropped close to his head, and the amber-coloured eyes. 'You're the best guide they have, I believe you told me,' she added with a touch of humour in her voice.

'You shouldn't have paid too much attention to what I said,' he replied, looking a little flushed as they negotiated the last of the steps before stepping on to the sandy beach. 'Like most people there that night I had had too much to drink,' he explained.

'You hid the fact well.'

He glanced at her, and she could see that he was a little uncertain of himself. 'Do you think so?'

'I would have said you were normally an arrogant, self-opinionated young man,' she remarked, tongue in cheek. 'I would never have attributed it to the amount of alcohol you'd consumed.'

A rueful expression flitted across his lean face. 'I didn't make a very good impression, did I?'

'I'm teasing you, Mr Pienaar,' she laughed now.

'Dirk,' he corrected. 'May I call you Jennifer?'

'You may.'

'Will you join me at my table for dinner this evening, Jennifer?'

'Do you usually work this fast?' she asked humorously, slanting a glance at his smiling face.

'Only when I think I might lose out if I waited.'

'May I give you an answer a little later?'

'I'll try to be patient,' he grinned.

Jennifer took off her sandals and carried them in her hand, enjoying the feel of the warm sand beneath her bare feet as they walked along in silence for a while.

'What are you doing here in Plettenberg Bay?' she asked at last.

'I'm on a week's leave.' His amber eyes were narrowed against the sun when they met hers. 'And you? What are you doing here?'

'We're stopping overnight on our way back to Oudt-shoorn.'

'We?' he questioned at once. 'You're here with Hunter Maynard and his mother?'

'Yes,' she nodded.

His face fell. 'I don't suppose I stand a chance, then, do I?'

'A chance to what?'

'To persuade you to join me for dinner.'

Making a spur-of-the-moment decision, she said: 'You've persuaded me already.'

'I have?' he asked, his face lighting up. 'Well, good for me!'

'I must go back to the hotel,' she said eventually, glancing at her wrist watch.

'Aren't you going for a swim?' Dirk asked disappointedly.

She shook her head. 'I didn't bring a swimsuit with me.'

'I'll walk you back to the hotel, then.'

'There's no need for you to do that,' she said at once, taking in his lean youthfulness in swimming briefs, towelling shirt, and beach towel slung casually over one shoulder. 'I would much rather you went for your swim.'

His glance mirrored uncertainty. 'If you're sure . . .'

'Of course I'm sure,' she insisted firmly. 'When and where shall I meet you for dinner?'

'In the foyer at seven.'

'I'll be there,' she smiled.

They parted company, and while he headed towards the crowded swimming area, she strolled back to the hotel, which stood out like a beacon against the azure blue sky. She had agreed to have dinner with Dirk Pienaar, which had perhaps been a mistake, but she could not sit through another embarrassing meal watching Louella making the most of her time with Hunter.

'Jennifer!' a harsh, familiar voice stopped her when she reached the patio, and she turned to see Hunter straightening from his leaning position against the low wall. His corded pants hugged his slim hips and muscular thighs, while his white shirt strained across the wide expanse of his shoulders, and her breath became locked in her throat at the sight of him. 'Who was that you were talking to on the beach?'

Her hackles rose at once at his abrupt query. 'I can't see that it's any business of yours, but his name is Dirk Pienaar.'

'Dirk Pienaar?' he echoed sharply.

'He's a guide at the Cango Caves in Oudtshoorn,' Jennifer refreshed his memory, and his eyes narrowed dangerously.

'I'm well aware of that.'

'May I go now?' she asked, her defiant glance meeting his. 'Or was there something else you wanted to know?'

For a moment he did not speak, then he stepped away from the wall and lessened the distance between them. 'Mother has decided to have her dinner sent up to her room again this evening, so we'll be dining alone.'

'Correction, Hunter. *You* will be dining alone,' she replied coldly, shutting her mind and heart to the invitation which had lurked behind his statement as she added: 'I'm dining with Dirk.'

Hunter's jaw hardened. 'He hasn't wasted much time in propositioning you, has he?'

'No, he hasn't, and I must admit that I liked his style,' she taunted him deliberately, knowing only too well that she would hate herself afterwards.

'He's too young and inexperienced for you, Jennifer.'

'Oh, I don't think so,' she shrugged casually.

An icy hostility lurked in his deep blue eyes as he said derisively, 'Don't say that I didn't warn you if your evening ends in disappointment.'

As usual, his insinuating remarks penetrated her composure, and her eyes flashed green fire up at him. 'I'm seldom disappointed, but often disgusted, and right this minute you disgust me, Hunter Maynard.'

'Why?' he demanded mockingly. 'Because you haven't succeeded yet in making me believe that you possess the purity of a nun?'

She bit down hard on a lip that quivered with emotion. 'You may think what you damn well like!'

'I always do,' he assured her harshly as she turned to flee from him, 'and I'm seldom wrong.'

Her breathing was hard and uneven with the force of her anger when she reached her room. Just who did Hunter Maynard think he was! Right from the start he had sat in judgment on her, and he had given his verdict without so much as offering her the opportunity to defend herself. Granted, she had, in moments of anger, gone out of her way to make him believe the worst, but then he had had no business to condemn her outright.

It was with these disturbing and infuriating thoughts that Jennifer dressed for dinner that evening. She was glad now that she had accepted Dirk's invitation to dine with him and, after paying a courtesy call on Alice Maynard, she took the lift down into the foyer of the hotel.

'It looks like Mr Maynard is dining alone,' Dirk remarked when they saw Hunter being shown to a table some distance from theirs.

'So it seems,' she replied with a casualness she did not feel.

Dirk shifted uncomfortably in his chair and said tentatively, 'Should I ask him to join us?'

Her insides twisted into that familiar knot. 'Don't spoil my evening as well as my appetite, Dirk.'

'You sound as though you don't like him very much,' he observed with a touch of humour in his voice, and she gestured dismissingly.

'Let's talk about something else.'

Dirk took a sip of wine and smiled at her across the table. 'I believe they have some entertainment lined up for us this evening.'

'You're referring to the singer, Louella, I presume?'

Dirk nodded enthusiastically. 'I never saw her when she was in Oudtshoorn, but I believe she's quite luscious.'

'If you go for that kind of beauty, yes,' she replied dryly.

'You've seen her?' Dirk asked, eyeing her with surprise.

'She travelled with us from Port Elizabeth this morning,' Jennifer explained, wishing they could step off the subject.

'You know her, then?'

'Hunter knows her,' she corrected distastefully.

'Oh,' said Dirk, the excitement in his eyes fading.

'Don't look like that,' she laughed.

'Like what?'

'Like a little boy who's had his favourite ice-cream swiped out of his hand,' she told him humorously.

'Just wait until I'm Hunter Maynard's age,' he announced, brightening swiftly. 'I'll dazzle the girls into a frazzle!'

Jennifer laughed softly. 'You're dazzling enough as it is, so simmer down, boy.'

Dirk's smile broadened. 'You sure make me feel good, Jennifer.'

Something, a force stronger than her own, made her glance across the room, and the smile froze on her lips when her eyes met the dark fury of Hunter's intent gaze. A cold little shiver travelled up her spine, and the waiter caused a welcome diversion at that moment to serve the meal they had ordered, but she could not shake off entirely the uneasiness which had taken hold of her.

She enjoyed Dirk's company, but that did not lessen her awareness of Hunter's formidable presence across the room from them, and the meal which Dirk had ordered with such care went down her throat like sawdust.

The band was playing softly in the background, but no one took much notice until Louella put in an appearance. In a crimson dress, more daring than the one she had worn the night before, she had the male audience at her feet, and there was a sudden hush when the lights were dimmed to capture Louella in the spotlight.

She followed the same routine, her husky voice exuding a sensual quality that matched the words of the song, but Jennifer was not paying her much attention. She was watching Dirk instead, and the expressions that flitted across his lean face were a great deal more interesting than the singer, or the song, Jennifer decided with some amusement.

Dirk was not impressed, and when Louella disappeared behind the green velvet curtains to the accompaniment of the enthusiastic applause, Jennifer succeeded in capturing his glance.

'Disappointed?' she asked, finding it difficult to suppress a smile.

'Oh, she's beautiful all right,' he conceded, 'but she reminds me of an over-ripe peach; still good to the taste, but rotten inside.'

Jennifer giggled, but Dirk was not finished yet with his analysis. 'I like blondes too, but not when their roots are black,' he elaborated and, glancing across the room to where Louella had now joined Hunter at his table, Dirk added: 'She doesn't strike me as Hunter Maynard's type either.'

'Oh, you'd be surprised,' Jennifer remarked, her voice heavy with sarcasm as she dragged her glance from the sight of Louella leaning across the table towards Hunter while they exchanged intimate smiles.

She tried not to glance in that direction again, but she could not help herself, and a wave of white-hot jealousy seared through her when she saw Hunter whisper something in Louella's ear which brought a dreamy smile to the singer's lips.

Jennifer wrenched her eyes from the sight to find herself shaking inwardly. She had never known jealousy before, let alone a jealousy as destructive as this, and she cringed inwardly at the suggestion which she imagined had brought that looked of intimate delight to Louella's strikingly attractive face.

'Shall we go for a walk on the beach?' Dirk suggested at length, and Jennifer grasped at the opportunity to get away like someone grasping at a lifeline.

'A short walk, yes,' she said as she rose from her chair and allowed Dirk to drape her wrap about her shoulders. 'I'd like to have an early night tonight.'

She was almost certain that Hunter watched them leave, she could feel his eyes boring into her back, and she filled her tortured lungs with fresh sea air when they stepped out on to the patio and turned towards the steps leading down on to the smooth, moonlit beach.

'Will I see you again when I return to Oudtshoorn at the end of the week?' Dirk asked when she had removed her high-heeled sandals to walk on stockinged feet across the cool, soft sand.

'I'm not sure,' she replied, dragging her thoughts back to the man beside her.

'What do you mean, you're not sure?' Dirk demanded. 'Don't you want to see me again?'

'It's not that,' she assured him hastily. 'I might have returned to Cape Town by that time.'

'Are you honestly leaving that soon?' he asked with disappointment clearly evident in his voice.

'Mrs Maynard is well enough to manage on her own now, and I've become rather superfluous,' she explained, swallowing down the lump which had risen unexpectedly in her throat.

'That means I might never see you again.'

Jennifer drew her gaze from the ever-moving sea to glance at him. 'Don't look so sad about it.'

'But I am.'

'You must know plenty of girls.'

He shrugged carelessly. 'I know a few, but——'

'But?' she prompted curiously.

'You're not going to believe this, but I'm usually so tonguetied with them that I seldom know what to talk about,' he confessed.

'But you haven't been tonguetied with me,' she argued.

'You're not young and silly.'

'You make me feel like a grandmother,' she said reprovingly, and he looked faintly embarrassed when she stopped to face him squarely.

'I didn't mean it that way,' he assured her, 'but the girls I know are all just out of their teens, and you're . . . how old?'

She hid a smile of amusement. 'You shouldn't ask a woman her age, Dirk, but I'll be twenty-five next month.'

'We're the same age, then.'

'That's nice,' she murmured, unable to match his enthusiasm.

'Shall we go back?' he asked eventually, peering at her closely in the star-studded darkness.

'I think so.'

He took her hand and drew it through his arm as they strolled back along the deserted beach towards the hotel, and they walked in silence for a time until he said curiously, 'Tell me, Jennifer, did Hunter have any objections about you having dinner with me?'

She stiffened automatically. 'I'm a free agent, Dirk, and I can have dinner with whom I please.'

'You should have seen the glowering looks he shot in your direction before that Louella woman joined him at his table,' he laughed softly.

'I couldn't care less how he looked at me,' she replied coldly, but it was not true. She did care, she cared very much, and she would have given anything for him to smile at her just once in the way he had smiled at Louella.

'I've heard a rumour that he's going to marry Carla von Brandis,' Dirk's voice invaded her thoughts. 'Is this true?'

'I wouldn't know,' she lied. 'Why do you ask?'

'I just wondered, because I've seen her a couple of times with Hunter's cousin Stanley, cuddling around corners at functions, and so on.' After what she had witnessed personally, this no longer had the power to shock her, she discovered as she felt Dirk shrug beside her. 'If you ask me, she's playing Hunter for a sucker.'

Jennifer considered this in silence for a time, then she said quietly, 'I guess it's really none of our business, Dirk.'

'No, I suppose it isn't,' he agreed, and they continued their walk in silence, but when they reached the hotel foyer he turned her round to face him and gripped her hands tightly. 'Do you have to go now?'

She looked up into his amber-coloured eyes and nodded. 'I'm tired, Dirk, but it's been a lovely evening, and I've really enjoyed your company.'

'I shan't forget you in a hurry.'

'Oh, yes, you will,' she smiled and, extricating her hands gently from his, she said: 'Goodbye, Dirk.'

'I prefer to say *tot siens*,' he returned her smile a little sadly. 'It doesn't sound so final.'

Jennifer did not reply to that, but when she stepped into the lift she turned to see that he was still standing where she had left him. He raised his hand in a swift salute before the doors slid shut, and then she was being swept up to the sixth floor.

A tiredness seeped into her limbs; a tiredness which seemed to stem from a heavy-laden heart. In less than a week she would be returning to Cape Town, and she would, no doubt, never see Hunter again. She did not want to think of it; she wanted to think of Dirk instead, but her mind conjured up the torturous vision of a lonely, empty future, and she groaned inwardly when she stepped from the lift to walk the short distance to her room. She had thought that she would never recover from Colin's death, and yet she had, but only to learn the real meaning of love; a love in which there was no future. Hunter would never believe anything but the worst of her, and she supposed that she was partially to blame for the opinion he had formed of her. He needed to trust again, to regain his faith in women, but he would never find what he was seeking with Carla, and most certainly not with Louella.

'That's what I like about women like Louella. They don't pretend to be what they're not,' Hunter's words echoed through her mind.

Jennifer could almost understand and sympathise. He knew what kind of woman Louella was, and he admired her for not denying it, but his admiration and faith in women ended right there.

Her mind was in a painful turmoil when she took her keys from her purse and unlocked her bedroom door, but, when she closed it behind her moments later and switched on the light, her heart lurched with a paralysing fear.

'Hunter!' she exclaimed hoarsely as he uncurled his great length from the high-backed chair facing the glass doors which led out on to the balcony.

'Surprised to see me?' he asked mockingly as he turned to face her, his razor-sharp glance raking over her pale features unsympathetically.

It took several agonising seconds for her to recover sufficiently from the shock of finding him there, and when she spoke her voice still bore traces of the nervous tremor which had not quite subsided within her.

'What are you doing here?' she managed huskily.

'Waiting for you,' he smiled faintly.

Her eyes darted about the room. 'How did you get in?'

'The door on to your balcony was open, and our balconies

are linked by a low wall,' he explained casually. 'It was a simple matter just to climb over it.'

Jennifer pushed herself away from the door which had acted as a support to keep her upright on her trembling limbs and, making a tremendous effort to appear calm, she removed her wrap and placed it with her evening purse and keys on the table against the wall.

'What do you want?' she asked, her voice much steadier now.

'To talk to you.'

Suspicion was mirrored in her eyes. 'What about?'

'About your evening spent with Dirk Pienaar,' he elaborated smoothly. 'Were you disappointed?'

She clamped down hard on her rising temper, and said, 'No, I was not.'

'You mean, he gained by your experience, and in that way he made the evening worthwhile for you?'

His mocking insinuations sliced deep, but still she hung on to her temper as she met his glance unwaveringly. 'Hunter, I'm tired, and I'm in no mood to enter into a verbal battle with you.'

'A verbal battle wasn't exactly what I had in mind.'

Those hard, glittering eyes held hers captive while his statement took time to sink into her lethargic brain, then she wrenched open the door and said icily, 'Get out!'

'Not so fast,' he replied, moving with incredible speed to slam the door shut before she even had it open properly. With her hand still clutching the handle the force of his actions dragged her with it so that she landed somehow with her back against the carved doorframe to find Hunter towering over her in a frightening manner. 'I intend to have my fair share of the takings,' he told her harshly.

'What—what do you mean?' she demanded hesitantly,

not wanting to accept the warning her mind shouted out to her.

'Just what I said,' he replied, his jaw hard and unrelenting. 'It's my turn tonight.'

Fear trickled up her spine, chilling the blood in her veins, but she was determined not to show it. 'What happened to Louella? Is she occupied elsewhere this evening?'

His eyes burned down into hers, and his lips were drawn back in anger against his strong teeth. 'Forget about Louella.'

'Why should I when you're so damned interested in whom I spend my time with, and how?' Her voice had risen in anger and fear. 'You accuse me of having no morals, but what about yourself?'

'Shut up!' he ordered menacingly.

'I won't shut up!' she cried, but when she saw the dangerous gleam in his eyes she knew that anger would not come to her rescue on this occasion and, passing a tired hand over her eyes, she said with a forced calmness, 'Please, Hunter, don't contemplate anything you'll end up regretting in the morning.'

'I shan't regret it, I assure you.' She stood impassively beneath his hands as they caressed her throat and shoulders before brushing aside the narrow straps of her dress, and his touch sent a strange fire racing through her veins which quickened her pulse. His eyes darkened, the pupils enlarging, and his rough voice held a note of unmistakable desire when he said: 'I want you, Jenny, and I mean to have you.'

She wished that she could run from him, and from this fatal magnetism he exuded, but her tired limbs refused to move, and she realised that her only escape lay in the hope that she could perhaps reason with him.

'If this is intended as some sort of joke, Hunter, then

don't you think it's gone far enough?' she asked unsteadily, her breath coming fast over parted lips.

'This is no joke, Jenny,' he assured her, 'and neither is this.'

His hands slid down her back, moulding her into the curve of his body while his hard mouth bruised hers with a savage passion that seared her soul, and stirred up an answering fire she could not suppress. Fear was the only thing that made her cling to her sanity as she struggled wildly against him in an effort to escape, but the bruising pressure of his mouth increased, and his arms tightened about her crushingly, leaving her no room to breathe, or think, or even stop to consider Carla.

A blackness threatened to engulf her as he edged her towards the bed, and his mouth left hers only briefly as he lowered her on to it, giving her the much needed opportunity to draw air into her lungs, but his lips swooped down on to hers again almost as if he had anticipated the cry that rose in her throat. She struggled beneath him, conscious of lean hips and muscled thighs pressing into hers as he pulled down the zip of her dress, but her efforts to escape were futile, and those clever hands against her responsive flesh drove away the last shred of her sanity until there was only the aching desire to belong to him.

The shrill ringing of the telephone on the bedside table sliced through her dulled senses and acted like a douche of iced water. She dragged her lips from Hunter's, but strong fingers latched on to her wrist, staying her hand in the act of reaching for the receiver.

'Leave it!' he ordered in a voice still vibrant with passion.

'It could be something important,' she pleaded, frantic now as his tongue explored her ear and travelled sensuously down to the rosy peak of her breast to send delicious little shivers cascading through her receptive body.

'Nothing could be more important than this at the moment,' he growled.

'Hunter, please!' she begged, her breath coming fast and uneven over parted lips, and her hands pushing frantically at his shoulders. 'It might be your mother.'

The mention of his mother seemed to have a sobering effect on him at last, and he rolled away from her with a muttered oath on his lips, giving her the opportunity to restore some order to her appearance while he lifted the receiver off the hook and extended it towards her.

'Hello? Hello? Are you there, Jennifer?' Alice Maynard's voice could be heard quite distinctly, and Jennifer almost snatched the receiver from his hand.

'Yes, Mrs Maynard?' she said into the mouthpiece, but even to her own ears her voice sounded strange.

'Is something wrong?' Alice demanded at once.

From the gleam of mockery in Hunter's eyes Jennifer knew that he could hear every word his mother was saying, and she made a decisive effort to pull herself together as she said haltingly, 'No . . . no, of course not.'

Alice seemed to hesitate, then she sighed and said: 'Look, Jennifer, I know it's late, but do you think you could come along and give my leg a massage?'

'I'm coming at once, Mrs Maynard,' Jennifer replied, then a shiver of emotion rippled through her as Hunter trailed a sensual finger up her spine in the process of pulling up her zip.

She replaced the receiver hastily and rose jerkily to her feet, placing a suitable distance between Hunter and herself before she felt capable of facing him.

'That was your mother,' she said unnecessarily.

'So I heard,' he answered abruptly, and not without a thread of anger in his voice.

Their eyes met and held; his searching and intent, hers wary, and something in the way his mouth hardened compelled her to say, 'You would have regretted it, Hunter.'

It was a mistake to say that, for his eyes travelled over her with a slow sensuality that made her tremble as if he had actually touched her physically, and intimately, and the blood rushed painfully into her cheeks when he smiled with faint satisfaction and said: 'I don't somehow think so.'

She came to her senses as if he had slapped her and, walking towards the door, she fought to regain her composure. Her hand was as cold as the chrome handle, and opening the door wide, she said: 'Please go.'

Hunter crossed the room until he stood directly in front of her, and the height and breadth of him set her nerves quivering once more. His eyes were hard, as hard as the line of his square jaw, and a little shiver of apprehension coursed its way through her.

'What will you do if I insist on waiting here for you to return?'

'I shall think up some plausible excuse to spend the night in your mother's room,' she replied without hesitation, and his eyebrows rose in sardonic amusement.

'You won't always escape me this easily, Jennifer,' he warned. 'Next time I shall have what I came for.'

Something in his manner made her aware of how vulnerable she was, and how totally she would be at his mercy if he should actually carry out his threat, and her anger rose sharply, her eyes sparking green fire as she raised them to his.

'I'll see you in hell first!' she hissed.

'I accept that as a challenge,' he nodded abruptly. 'Good-night, Jennifer.'

He strode down the passage, his footsteps making no sound on the thick pile of the carpet, and her eyes, frightened now, followed him until he was out of sight.

Was he serious, or was he merely trying to frighten her? If he were confronted with the truth would he change his opinion of her, or would he scorn her? These questions, unanswered, raced through her mind, but whichever way she looked at it, there was only one thing she could do to avoid the final humiliation of having him learn the truth, and that was to leave Vogelsvlei as soon as possible. If Hunter succeeded in carrying out his threat he would discover that she loved him, and that was something she dared not allow. Knowing it, he would destroy her, and she would never be able to live with herself after that.

CHAPTER NINE

JENNIFER put on a more comfortable pair of shoes and slipped into one of her overalls before going along to Alice Maynard's room to massage her leg and hip. Her hip had healed well, but it was not yet strong enough to take the long hours of travelling which they had accomplished since leaving Vogelsvlei early the previous day. Jennifer's mind was somehow not on what she was doing, and Hunter's behaviour had disturbed and frightened her, making the level of her uneasiness rise sharply.

'I hope you don't mind my calling you at this late hour?' Alice asked tentatively, her eyes searching Jennifer's.

'I don't mind at all, Mrs Maynard,' she assured the older woman at once. 'I hadn't gone to bed yet, and even if I had it wouldn't have mattered.'

'You're an angel of mercy, Jennifer. I've been in agony most of the afternoon and evening.'

Jennifer glanced up sharply from her task. 'You should have called me in sooner. I wouldn't have minded, you know that, and I was, after all, employed specifically to help you.'

'I know, I know,' Alice muttered impatiently, 'but I didn't want to spoil things for you. You deserved this little break from your usual routine.'

'You've always given me plenty of freedom, and I've appreciated that, but if you should need me while I'm still with you, then you mustn't hesitate to call me.'

Alice laughed shortly. 'You sound just like Marian when

you speak to me in that tone of voice; reprimanding and authoritative.'

'I presume you're speaking of Matron Griffiths,' Jennifer smiled down at her. 'Your sister is a very good Matron, and I certainly don't envy her the responsibility that goes with her job.'

'Don't think that I'm not fond of my sister, Jennifer,' Alice said at once. 'I know I quite often utter a few disparaging remarks which are directed at her, but it's because I know how much she has had to change to fit the position she holds. She's really a very tenderhearted soul, but . . .' Alice smiled mischievously '. . . don't let her know I said so.'

'I won't,' Jennifer laughed, but her laughter was stifled in her throat the next instant.

'You looked disturbed when you came in just now,' Alice was saying. 'Was it Hunter? Has he upset you again?'

Jennifer lowered her glance hastily and concentrated on making Alice comfortable as she said: 'Your son and I somehow don't get on together.'

'You saw him just before I telephoned you?'

'Briefly, yes,' Jennifer lied, not wanting Mrs Maynard to know what had transpired between Hunter and herself.

'I thought there was something wrong when I spoke to you on the telephone,' Alice concluded thoughtfully. 'You sounded quite odd.'

'I think you should get some rest now,' Jennifer changed the subject hastily, hoping Alice did not notice the pinkness of her cheeks.

'I'm looking forward to tomorrow's trip home,' Alice sighed. 'We shall at least be rid of that dreadful Louella woman.'

Would they really be rid of her? Jennifer wondered when she eventually turned out the light and left Alice Maynard's room. Or could they expect Louella to turn up at Vogelsvlei some time in the not too distant future?

Jennifer tried to shrug off these thoughts, but she did not succeed entirely, and her dreams were fraught with visions of Hunter coming to her from Louella's arms, and forcing an entry into her room. He wanted her, he said, and she could not escape the sensual touch of his hands against her skin, arousing her to a physical desire that filled her with an aching need, but she screamed when he shifted his body over hers, and she awoke to find herself alone in her bed with the dawn sky banishing the shadows of the night.

Perspiration stood out on her forehead, and she had difficulty in controlling her sobbing breath. It had been a dream, but it had been so real that she could almost swear her body still tingled with the memory of his touch. Furious with herself, she got out of bed and went through to the bathroom to drink a little water, but deep shadows lurked beneath the eyes that met hers in the mirror above the basin, while fear and pain lurked in their hazel depths. She could not remain at Vogelsvlei a moment longer than was necessary, and, with Dr Tremayne's permission, she would return to Cape Town as soon as possible.

Jennifer felt much better after taking a cool, refreshing shower, then she changed into a cool summer frock and packed her suitcase in readiness for their departure after breakfast that morning.

The journey back to Vogelsvlei was accomplished without incident, except that the interior of Hunter's Mercedes still reeked with Louella's perfume, and they had not travelled far that morning when Alice Maynard sneezed several times. She muttered something uncomplimentary about it being enough to give anyone a severe attack of sinus, and then she opened the window to such an extent that the air blowing into the car almost threatened to tear the pins from Jennifer's hair where she sat beside Hunter.

Out of the corner of his eye he noticed her silent efforts to keep her hair in place and, speaking over his shoulder, he ordered sharply, 'Close your window, Mother. The air-conditioner will have a better effect that way.'

'I sincerely hope it does,' she muttered, but Hunter paid no attention while he concentrated on the road and flicked the appropriate switches on the dashboard to allow a cool draught of refreshing air into the car.

His hand accidentally brushed against Jennifer's knee, and although he appeared not to have noticed, a tingling awareness had shot up her leg. It was this awareness which made her shrink farther into the corner of her seat and, for the duration of their journey, she kept her eyes riveted to the lush coastal scenery before they headed northwards in the direction of Oudtshoorn.

One of the first things Jennifer did after their arrival at Vogelsvlei was to telephone Dr Tremayne to determine his medical opinion on whether he considered it necessary for her to remain much longer with Alice Maynard.

'I've just spoken to the specialist in Port Elizabeth, and he has confirmed my diagnosis,' Dr Tremayne informed her. 'Mrs Maynard is quite mobile, and there's no reason at all why you should remain at Vogelsvlei if you wish to return to Cape Town.'

Jennifer was relieved to hear this, and yet she was sad. She had grown fond of Alice Maynard and this marvellous old house. She would miss the ostriches too, she thought as she strolled down towards the nearest camp without actually realising where she was going.

She leaned her elbows on the fence and sighed un-happily, recalling that day she had been idiotic enough to rush into this very camp to rescue her scarf. She had never worn that bright scarf again, but each time she had encountered it in her drawer it had acted as a humiliating reminder of her foolishness. Hunter had had every right to be furious with her, she thought, and she sighed once more as her glance travelled towards the beautiful male ostrich running slowly and daintily on the point of his toes while in pursuit of his female. His long neck, upright and rigid, was slightly inflated, and with his tail drooping slightly, but with his black body feathers fluffed up, he was an extremely beautiful bird.

'The male is courting the female,' Hunter's deep voice spoke directly behind her, and her nerves coiled themselves into tight knots when he rested his arms on the fence beside her. 'The ostrich is a patient lover. He takes his time courting the female, and he literally degenerates himself in his efforts to win her favours.'

Jennifer smothered the frightening suspicion that he was not referring to the ostriches entirely, but the next instant Hunter was drawing her attention back to the male ostrich.

She witnessed, not for the first time, the male ostrich bumping down in its knees, opening its wings to form a straight line across his chest, and then swinging backwards and forwards, keeping in that straight line. His neck was lowered until his head was level with his back as he swung his head and neck from side to side with his wings, and the back of his head would strike against the ribs on either side with a loud 'click'.

'That's what you call "rolling",' Hunter explained quietly. 'They do that when they're challenging another male to a fight, or when they're courting. On this occasion it's obvious that his interest lies in the female standing a little distance away from him with her head down, and her wings spread out to tempt him, but that's no assurance that she will eventually accept his advances.'

While Jennifer watched with bated breath, the male ostrich rose to his feet once more and tripped lightly and gracefully towards the female, but, temperamentally, she warded off his advances with a flap of her wings, and moved away towards the opposite side of the camp. The male, however, lost none of his dignity, and with a display of total uninterest, he continued grazing in the lucerne field.

'The scene is different, but the action is familiar, don't you agree?'

His taunting remark sent a wave of colour into her cheeks and, turning away from his disturbing nearness, she said coolly, 'I don't know what you're talking about.'

'I can recall at least two occasions when my advances were warded off,' he continued to mock her, falling into step beside her as she walked back to the house.

She flashed an angry glance at him, and said sarcastically, 'I had no idea that you were courting me, Hunter. If I had known, I might have been more receptive.'

'I shall remember that, you little vixen,' he threatened with a harsh laugh, reaching for her, but she stepped aside smartly to avoid that tanned, muscled arm.

'I think Agnes is calling us for lunch,' she changed the subject, and quickened her pace as she crossed the lawn with Hunter matching his long strides to hers.

Several times during lunch that day, Jennifer encountered Hunter's gaze resting intently on her person, and it filled her with renewed anxiety. She could no longer delay her departure, she was certain of that, but at the same time she could not shake off her reluctance to broach the subject with Alice Maynard.

It was a warm, mid-spring day, but instead of resting in her room, Jennifer took a magazine out into the garden with her, and made herself comfortable on the wooden bench beneath the shady trees. She paged through the magazine for quite some time, not actually taking in what she was reading, when Carla's small red car swept up the drive, and crunched to a halt a little distance from her. Half hidden behind the shrubs, Jennifer went unnoticed, but her heart missed a beat when Hunter appeared as if from nowhere to witness Carla's arrival. In a panic, Jennifer hovered between making her presence known, and remaining where she was as Carla leapt from her car to fling her arms about Hunter's neck.

'Hunter, darling!' she exclaimed ecstatically.

'Cut that out, Carla,' Hunter rebuked her sharply, removing her arms roughly from about his neck, and at this point Jennifer decided that it would be an unwise move to make it known that she was there.

'Well, that's a nice way to greet me, I must say!' Carla retorted angrily, flicking her long hair back over one shoulder as she faced up to Hunter. 'You should have been home yesterday, if I remember correctly. I've been worried sick about you, and here you are, treating me like a leper. Where have you been all this time?'

Through the shrubbery Jennifer could see Hunter's face darken with annoyance, and she held her breath automatically.

'I don't have to account to you for my actions, and where I've been is none of your business,' he told Carla with a harshness that surprised Jennifer when she considered that this was the girl he was supposed to marry.

'Don't you dare talk to me like that!' Carla spat out the words in a fury.

'I'll talk to you any damn way I please,' Hunter replied in an ominous voice. 'Now get in your car and go home. Or try out your wiles on Stanley. He might be a little more accommodating.'

He knows! Jennifer thought, a tremor of shock rippling through her. He *knows* about Carla and Stanley, and somehow she felt intensely relieved.

'I think I might just do that,' Carla's sarcastic reply sliced through Jennifer's thoughts. 'Stanley has always been more fun than you could ever be.'

'Then don't let me stop you, and in future I'd be grateful if you'd limit your little games to Stanley,' Hunter warned, irritation and anger mirrored on his hard features.

Jennifer held her breath once more when she saw Carla fling back her head to glare up at the tall man before her. 'I think I hate you, Hunter Maynard!'

'Sure, sure!' he replied with obvious impatience. 'Now be a good girl. Get in your car, and do as I say.'

He turned on his heel and strode angrily in the direction of the sorting room, leaving a furious Carla to stand staring after him. The moment he was out of sight Carla stamped her foot like a thwarted child, then she turned and marched towards her car, her steps short and angry.

Jennifer's hopes of remaining undetected were dashed the next instant, for when Carla reached her car her glance pivoted in Jennifer's direction and, with an angry exclamation on her lips, she walked across the lawn to where Jennifer was seated behind the shrubs.

'I suppose you heard all that?' she snapped her query, flames of anger darting from her dark eyes.

'I couldn't help but hear it,' Jennifer admitted with a sigh, rising to her feet to face Carla in all her fury.

'It's all your fault!'

Jennifer's eyes widened in shocked surprise. 'I beg your pardon?'

'You've been trying to take Hunter away from me since the day you arrived here,' Carla elaborated, spitting pure venom.

'That's not true, Carla.'

'I'm not stupid, you know,' she hissed. 'I've seen the way you look at him.'

Jennifer went hot, then cold, but her composure remained intact. 'I dare say you have,' she returned swiftly. 'Hunter is not the kind of man a woman could ignore, but then I've seen you with Stanley too, and I couldn't help wondering just what you were up to.'

She knew that she had scored a hit when Carla paled visibly, but those liquid-brown eyes lost none of their fire. 'What are you talking about?'

'If you need to have your memory refreshed, then it was at the Valley Motel last Saturday,' Jennifer explained. 'I went out into the garden for a breath of fresh air, and I saw the two of you together.'

'Yes, yes, I know about that!'

Carla seemed agitated now, and ill at ease.

'Well?' Jennifer prompted when the silence lengthened. 'Do you think you were being fair to Hunter?'

'It meant nothing,' Carla snapped. 'Stanley and I have always been . . . fond of each other, but when it came to marriage there was only one man for me, and now you've turned him against me.' Her beautiful eyes were now almost black as she hissed furiously, 'I could kill you for doing this to me!'

'Don't be silly, Carla,' Jennifer remonstrated with her calmly. 'I haven't taken Hunter away from you, and you know as well as I do that there could never be anything between us.'

'I don't know why you had to come here to Vogelsvlei,' Carla stormed at her. 'Everything was working out beautifully until you arrived. In fact, everything was working out exceptionally well until you went on this trip to Port Elizabeth.' Her angry eyes narrowed to slits of suspicion. 'What happened there?'

'Nothing happened.'

'Like *hell* nothing happened!' Carla shouted, looking Jennifer up and down in the most disdainful manner. 'Did he make love to you?'

The question was unexpected, and Jennifer's insides jerked violently, but she managed to remain outwardly calm, and her voice was cold as she said: 'Don't be absurd!'

They stood facing each other, like the enemy summing up the opposition, and neither of them wishing to give the order to retreat. The silence was tense, antagonistic, and lengthy, but it was Carla who finally had the last word.

With her hands clenched tightly at her sides of her quivering body, and venomous hatred flashing in her dark eyes, she hissed threateningly, 'You haven't heard the last of this, believe me, Jennifer Casey!'

Moments later her car was kicking up a cloud of dust as she sped away from Vogelsvlei, and only then did Jennifer realise what an effect this incident had had on her. Her legs were shaking, and her palms were damp, and deep inside her there was the aching knowledge that Hunter was aware of Carla's deceit. It was no wonder that he had no faith in women if Carla was an example of the female company he kept, Jennifer thought unhappily, and she wished desperately that there was something she could do about it. The worst part of it all was being accused of coming between Hunter and Carla. It was ludicrous to even think it! she told herself. She had never deliberately poached on Carla's preserves, but if this was what Carla thought, then there was all the more reason why she should leave Vogelsvlei as soon as possible, Jennifer thought.

She walked back to the house, intent upon asking Alice Maynard to release her, but when she found herself face to face with the older woman she somehow lacked the courage of her convictions. Perhaps later, she told herself. Not now; not just yet, she decided, and a little voice from somewhere said accusingly, '*Coward!*'

She cringed inwardly as the word bounced through her mind. She had never been a coward, but leaving Vogelsvlei meant leaving Hunter, and although she feared what he could do to her, she knew that she could never love another man the way she loved this rude, arrogant, impossible man who had done nothing but insult and humiliate her from the day she had set foot in Oudtshoorn.

No matter how much she tried, she could not forget the scene she had witnessed between Hunter and Carla, and neither could she forget the things Carla had accused her of. Was it possible that she could have come between them in some way? Impossible! Not in the way Carla had meant, Jennifer answered her own question. Hunter had tried to make love to her, yes, but his intentions had been aimed purely at humiliating her, and nothing more. Perhaps, when she was gone, things would return to normal at Vogelsvlei. It was possible, of course, that Carla had merely used Stanley in order to make Hunter jealous and, perhaps, she had succeeded.

Jennifer was still not quite sure what to do for the best when she made her way towards Alice Maynard's room after dinner that evening. Perhaps, if they could have a quiet chat together, it would help her come to some definite decision, but, when she hesitated in the passage outside Alice's bedroom, it was Hunter's harsh voice that prevented her from knocking and entering.

'Mother, I want you to release Jennifer from her duties,' he was saying. 'You no longer require her assistance in any way.'

There was a brief silence during which Jennifer was afraid they might hear the heavy beating of her heart through the door which stood slightly ajar, and then Alice was saying haughtily, 'I think I'm the best judge of that, don't you?'

'No, Mother,' Hunter contradicted sternly. 'On this issue I have the final say.'

Jennifer did not wait to hear more. She retraced her steps down the passage and hurried up the stairs to her room before they could discover that she had overheard their conversation. Pain seemed to sweep through her in wave after successive wave until she could have cried out with the agony of it. Hunter wanted her out of the way, he could not have made it clearer had he tried, and she was going to oblige him.

She glanced about her for a moment with pain-filled eyes, then she took down her suitcases and started to pack. To be doing something eased the pain, but she dreaded the long night which still lay ahead of her. Heaven only knew how she was going to get through it, and the many days and nights which still lay ahead of her.

'Oh, God!' she groaned, lowering herself on to her bed and burying her face in her trembling hands. She had never felt more like crying, but the tears would not come. They lodged in her throat, tightening like a vice until it was almost an agony to breathe, then she pulled herself together forcibly, and tried to concentrate on her packing.

She ought to feel grateful towards Hunter, she told herself at last. He had helped to make up her mind, and this time tomorrow she would have shaken off the dust of Vogelsvlei, but there was no pleasure in this thought, only pain, and the pain was something she would have to learn to live with. She had been a fool to love a man who had no need of her, and she supposed she deserved to suffer for it, but, God help her, she had not wanted it this way.

Jennifer went to bed that night, but she could not sleep. It was close to midnight when she heard Hunter's heavy footsteps in the passage. He often worked long hours at night in his study, and she could not recall how many nights she had lain awake, waiting to hear his footsteps before she finally went to sleep, but on this occasion it had the opposite effect on her. She could still hear his deep, harsh voice demanding her dismissal, and it hurt like the very devil.

Hunter did not join Jennifer and his mother for breakfast the following morning, and while a part of her regretted this, there was another part of her which said that it was for the best. Agnes told them that Hunter had had an early breakfast, and that he had left a message that he would not be back before lunch that day. Everything was, in fact, working out just the way Jennifer had wanted it, but when breakfast was finally over it took a great deal of courage to broach the subject which had been preying on her mind most of the night.

'Mrs Maynard,' Jennifer began, her voice hesitant at first, but gaining momentum as she went on, 'I'd like your permission to leave Vogelsvlei.'

The grey eyes that met Jennifer's were startled and

anxious. 'You're not thinking of returning to Cape Town already, are you?'

'I have to think of it at some time, or another, and what better time than this?' Jennifer said, forcing a smile to her unwilling lips.

'I wish you would consider staying on another week or two.'

Jennifer shook her head. 'You no longer need me, Mrs Maynard.'

'I meant you to stay on as my guest, and not in your nursing capacity,' Alice elaborated hopefully, but Jennifer declined adamantly and tactfully.

'It's kind of you to want me to stay longer, but I'm afraid I can't.'

A silence settled between them; a silence during which they were both occupied with their own unhappy thoughts, and Jennifer was on the point of repeating her request when Alice Maynard asked quietly,

'When did you want to leave?'

'This morning,' Jennifer replied firmly. 'Immediately, if it wouldn't inconvenience you.'

A strained silence prevailed once more, then the older woman smiled sadly. 'You sound as if you're in a hurry to be rid of me.'

'It's not that at all, Mrs Maynard, and you know it,' Jennifer assured her hastily, swallowing down the painful lump which had risen in her throat. 'I've been happy here working for you, and with you, but I'm anxious to get back to my old job.'

Grey eyes met Jennifer's with a searching intensity. 'Did we make your stay here a pleasant one?'

'You were very kind to me, Mrs Maynard.'

'And Hunter?'

Jennifer hesitated, but only briefly. 'Hunter never wanted me here in the first place, and I have no doubt he'll be relieved when I've left the farm.'

'Jennifer, my dear, I might as well be frank with you,' Alice sighed unhappily after a brief pause. 'I had such wonderful hopes that my son would see his future in you.'

Jennifer's eyes clouded with pain, and she lowered her glance hastily to the untouched cup of coffee on the table in front of her. 'I don't know what to say.'

'Have I embarrassed you?'

'A little,' Jennifer admitted, conscious of a warmth stealing into her pale cheeks. 'But only because it's so totally out of the question.'

'So it seems,' Alice sighed again. 'When I think of all the trouble I went to I could weep. I encouraged you to go out with Stanley and Dr Hoffman for the simple reason that I hoped it would make Hunter sit up and take notice. In Port Elizabeth I left the two of you alone in the hope that something would come of it, but instead he picked up that Louella woman.' That gentle face was tight-lipped with anger now. 'Quite honestly, Jennifer, if he weren't so big, I would have taken him and shaken him!'

Jennifer lowered her glance hastily once more and toyed with the teaspoon in her saucer. 'There could never be anything between Hunter and myself, Mrs Maynard.'

'I would have said you were ideal for him,' Alice insisted, and Jennifer had to blink away the moisture in her eyes.

'You were mistaken.'

An awkward silence settled between them, then the older woman placed her hand gently on Jennifer's arm. 'I hope my confession hasn't embarrassed you too much.'

There were tears in Jennifer's eyes now as she raised her

glance. 'It makes me happy to know that you thought so much of me.'

'I've grown very fond of you, my dear.' Her fingers tightened briefly on Jennifer's arm. 'I'm going to miss you dreadfully.'

'I'm going to miss you, too,' Jennifer confessed, swallowing convulsively and blinking away the tears in her eyes.

Alice released Jennifer's arm and reached for the bell. 'I'll send Agnes with a message to Hunter.'

'No, don't do that!' Jennifer begged hastily. 'I'd rather he didn't know that I'm leaving.'

Alice eyed her curiously, but with a hint of astonishment lurking in her grey glance. 'Do you mean that you want to leave without seeing him?'

'I would prefer it that way.'

'May I ask why?'

Jennifer shifted uncomfortably in her chair beneath the older woman's direct gaze. This was no time to be evasive, she realised, so she decided on the truth. 'Hunter has never made a secret of the fact that he despises me. He never wanted me here in the first place, and leaving here is going to be difficult enough without having his insults ringing in my ears.'

'Perhaps you're right,' Alice admitted at length, then a strange look flashed across her face. 'I can't wait to see his face, though, when he finds out that you're gone.'

Jennifer did not want to contemplate Hunter's reaction to her departure and, pushing back her chair, she rose to her feet. 'There are a few things I still have to pack before I'm ready to leave.'

'Shall I send Agnes up to help you?'

Jennifer shook her head. 'That won't be necessary, thank you.'

Upstairs in her room, a few minutes later, Jennifer packed the last of her possessions and fastened the catches on her suitcases. There was a lump in her throat that just would not go down and, after taking a last long look at the room in which she had had to discard so many of her hopes and desires, she picked up her suitcases and went downstairs.

Saying goodbye to Alice Maynard was not easy, but they both managed to keep their tears in check, which was more than could be said for Emily the cook, and Agnes, who had always been ready and willing when she had been needed. Jennifer shook hands with them, and then, impulsively, she hugged Alice Maynard before climbing into her Fiat and driving away.

Just beyond the lane of pepper trees she saw Danny emerge from one of the camps and walk towards the small truck he always drove around in. She could not leave without a word to him and, braking sharply, she turned down the window.

'Goodbye, Danny,' she called to him, 'and thank you for looking after my car so well.'

Danny approached her with the broad rim of his old felt hat pulled forward to shade his eyes from the sun, and Jennifer knew that she would always see him that way in her thoughts.

'Are you leaving Vogelsvlei, *nonnie*?' he asked with a certain amount of astonishment.

'I'm returning to Cape Town,' she confessed, and Danny was clearly taken aback.

'We'll miss you, Nonnie Jennifer.'

That was so typical of Danny, she thought. There was no elaborate display of regret, just a simple statement which she knew came direct from his heart. She knew him that way, and she would remember him that way too.

'I'll miss you all,' she confessed, but in her heart she finished off the statement with, 'but I'll miss Hunter most of all.'

She eased her foot off the clutch and accelerated, and with a last wave of her hand she left Danny standing beside his truck. There were tears in her eyes, almost too many for her to see where she was going, but she could not stop; she dared not—not yet!

When she reached the main road she pulled off to the side and switched off the car's engine for a moment. She could not see Vogelsvlei's homestead from there, but she knew more or less where it lay and, drying her eyes, she stared in that direction for a long time. She would soon be on her way to Cape Town, but she had left an irretrievable part of her behind with a man who had no use for it. He had her heart in the palm of his hand, and he was crushing it cruelly. He had not asked for her love, but she had given it, and once given, she could never take it back.

Tears filled her eyes once more, but she brushed them away with the back of her hand in a gesture of irritation and anger. She would perhaps never come this way again, so she had better take one last look at the countryside before continuing on her way back, for once she had started the car there would be no looking back. The past would be behind her, and that was where it would stay. She had to face the future, and she would have to be strong. She would, eventually, find her solace in work, and she would have to learn to live with this new pain.

A car hooted loudly at two ostriches which were being driven across the road, and the sound jerked her out of her mood of self-pity and misery. She turned the key in the ignition and, without a backward glance, drove back the way she had come a little more than two months ago.

CHAPTER TEN

JENNIFER'S first weekend in Cape Town was utterly miserable. It rained all the time, forcing her to stay indoors, and she found that the loneliness and emptiness she had envisaged had now become a reality. She had delayed contacting Matron Griffiths, deciding that she was not yet ready to return to work, but being confined to her flat during this wet weekend was sheer agony. She had to do something to keep herself busy, or go quietly mad with longing, so she cleaned out the flat and tidied the cupboards. When that was done, she waxed the furniture with unusual vigour and concentration, and cleaned the silver. Anything was better than sitting around brooding and longing for something she could not have, and her extensive training did not include nursing an aching heart.

She made herself something to eat on the Sunday evening, but, like every other meal she had prepared for herself since her return, it turned to sawdust in her mouth, so she scraped it into a bowl for the neighbour's cat, washed the dishes, and packed them neatly into the cupboard. The flat had never been so tidy in all the years she had lived there, she decided cynically when she tried to settle down in the lounge with an out-of-date magazine, but it lay unopened in her lap while her mind darted backwards and forwards over the one subject she wanted so desperately to avoid.

Hunter! What was he doing? Had he been angered by her sudden departure, or had he been relieved? She presumed it was the latter, but that thought merely increased the ache in her heart. He despised her, and yet, on two specific occasions, he had wanted her. She could not understand it even now, and perhaps she never would. He was rude, arrogant, and insulting, she told herself in an effort to assuage the pain, but if she had to choose where she wanted most to be at that moment, she would choose to be with him.

'Oh, God, help me!' she groaned aloud, and flinging the magazine aside she went to the telephone and dialled Mike Hoffman's number out of sheer desperation. She needed someone to talk to, and Mike was the only one who would understand at that moment.

Mike arrived twenty minutes later and eased his lean frame on to the small sofa beside her, but his keen, dark glance did not miss the bruised look beneath her eyes, nor the shadows that lurked in their hazel depths.

'Things didn't work out so well with Hunter, I take it,' he observed calmly, and she shook her head, biting down hard on a quivering lip.

'The situation became impossible.'

With a cheerfulness for which she could willingly have throttled him, Mike said: 'Oh, well, there are still plenty of fish in the sea.'

'There'll never be another like Hunter Maynard.'

Mike sobered at once. 'It's like that, is it?'

'It's like that,' she confirmed, and for the first time since leaving Vogelsvlei she felt like bursting into tears.

'Bear up, sweetheart,' he said gently, placing a comforting arm about her shoulders. 'Old Mike's still here, and if you ever need a shoulder to cry on, just call and I'll come running.'

Taking him at his word, she lowered her head on to his shoulder and wept unrestrainedly into the handkerchief he

pressed into her hands. He comforted her, but wisely let
her cry until she felt drained and curiously at peace.

'You've helped me out of plenty of scrapes in the past,
and you've stood by me in difficult times,' she said eventually when she had wiped away her tears, and was in control
of herself once more. 'I don't know if I've ever told you how
much I've appreciated it, and still do.'

'Isn't that what friends are for?' he asked with a smile
of understanding in his dark eyes, and she leaned forward
to kiss him spontaneously on the cheek.

'You're sweet, Mike, and you've always been so very
good to me.'

'I also happen to be very thirsty,' he brushed aside her
remarks. 'Do you think you could rustle up a cup of
coffee?'

Jennifer smiled shakily and went through to the kitchen.
It was good to be doing something, she did not mind what,
and she felt a great deal better when she eventually returned to the lounge with their coffee.

'Are you going back to the General?' Mike asked at
length.

'For a time, yes, but I do feel I need a change.'

'I'm looking for a good receptionist-cum-nursing Sister.'
He eyed her speculatively. 'Will you consider it?'

Jennifer smiled. 'I might just surprise you and pitch up
at your consulting-rooms one morning.'

Mike remained with her for quite some time. He talked
about his work, about the rooms he had acquired where his
patients could consult him, and he finally had her laughing
at herself when he recounted the times he had had to save
her from the wrath of her superiors when she had still been
a student nurse.

Those had been good times, Jennifer recalled when Mike

had gone. They had been a carefree bunch; they had taken their nursing seriously, but they had also had a lot of fun. The difficult times had come later, when responsibilities had curtailed their often childish pranks, and then there had been Colin. His death had been a blow from which she had thought she would never recover, and yet she had. It had taken a rude, arrogant man like Hunter Maynard to put her back into life's orbit, but in the process she had laid herself wide open to the heartache which was now tearing her insides apart.

She must not think about it, she told herself sternly. She would get over it if she tried, but her mind showed her no mercy, for it conjured up a vision of Hunter's harsh features, his eyes mocking, and his smile taunting. She pressed her fingertips against her eyelids, trying desperately to blot out his image, but it remained with her, bringing back the pain and the longing, and the hopeless yearning for the impossible.

Hunter was not the kind of man one could forget easily, she realised yet again when she eventually went to bed to lie staring into the darkness with pain-filled eyes, but somehow she would have to succeed in her efforts. It would take time to wrench him from her heart and her mind, she told herself, but something warned her that she was contemplating the impossible. Time might ease the pain, but it could never erase the memory.

Jennifer telephoned Matron Griffiths at the hospital on the Monday morning, hoping to make an appointment to see her at some time during the day, but Matron Griffiths sounded rather vague at first, and then quite adamant that she could see her only the following day. Jennifer found it rather strange. She knew Matron Griffiths as a clear-thinking, decisive person, but she resigned herself eventually to the fact that she would have to face yet another day with nothing to do but fight her way through the hours.

The sun came out for the first time that morning since her return to Cape Town, and Jennifer took the opportunity to go out and buy a few necessary things. She took her time, but walking about idly was not something she enjoyed, and she arrived back at her flat within less than an hour to face the rest of the day alone. She had been given a taste, these last few days, of how lonely and empty her life was going to be in the future, and it was something she could not bear thinking about. There would, perhaps, be a certain amount of solace in work for her, but she could not work twenty-four hours a day, and heaven only knew what she was going to do with the hours she would have to herself.

The day dragged by, each hour like an eternity of agonising torture until she felt sure she would go mad if she did not find something to occupy her mind. Hunter, Hunter, Hunter! Like a faulty record she could think of nothing else. With every beat of her heart the longing grew more intense until it settled like a lead weight in her breast, weighing her down, and reducing her to a tearful, listless object which she was beginning to despise.

'Pull yourself together, Jennifer Casey!' she told herself sharply when at last the setting sun etched Table Mountain like a magnificent monument against the darkening sky, and she continued to reprimand herself in this manner as she went through to her small kitchen to prepare a light meal for herself.

She was not hungry, but she forced herself to eat, and washed it down later with a strong cup of coffee. The long night lay ahead of her like a threatening shadow, but she dared not think of it, and she concentrated instead on washing the dishes and tidying up the kitchen.

It was well after eight that evening when someone leaned heavily on the doorbell and, relieved at the thought that Mike had decided to drop in, Jennifer hurried through the lounge to let him in. It was not Mike, however, whom she found standing on her doorstep, and her welcoming smile froze on her lips.

'Hunter!' she breathed his name in a voice that sounded raw with suppressed emotion and, without waiting for an invitation, he pushed past her into the lounge and slammed the door behind him. He was so tall, so broad, and so exquisitely vital that he seemed to dwarf the room, and her heart was beating so fast that she could hardly breathe when she met the full impact of his ferocious glance. 'Who gave you my address?' she asked with difficulty.

'My aunt kindly supplied it from her files at the hospital,' he bit out the words, then he flung a large, curious-looking flat box into the nearest chair, and turned back to face her with a look on his harsh face that sent a familiar shiver of fear racing through her. 'You had no right to leave Vogelsvlei without consulting me,' he rasped accusingly.

Jennifer stared up at him for a moment, feasting her eyes on the man who had become so vital to her existence, and it was at that moment that she realised there was something different about him. He looked drawn and tired, with eyes that showed signs of lack of sleep, but this was no time to wonder at the reason, for his jaw was hardening with angry impatience.

'I discussed my departure with your mother, and that was sufficient, I thought,' she replied, moving away from his awe-inspiring nearness on legs that felt like jelly.

'So you left without so much as a goodbye,' he concluded harshly, following her across the room and giving her no time to regain her much needed composure.

'It was best that way.'

'Best for whom?'

'For all of us.'

'That was your opinion, of course,' he snarled at her.

What was he trying to do? she wondered when she found the courage to face him once more. Was he trying to destroy her? Her eyes travelled over him with barely concealed hunger, and there was that raw masculinity about him that never failed to stir her senses in a way that always alarmed her. The burning intensity of his eyes frightened her suddenly and, terrified of what he might see, she lowered her lashes.

'Stop splitting hairs, Hunter!' she exclaimed, resorting to anger as her only defence. 'If you hadn't made it quite clear to me before that I was unwelcome in your home, then you certainly succeeded on my last night at Vogelsvlei. I heard you telling your mother that you wanted me dismissed from my duties, and in the light of that information I didn't consider it necessary to consult you, nor to ask your permission to remove my unwanted presence from your farm.'

'Dammit, Jennifer, I could shake you!' His hands bit into her shoulders as if he was going to carry out his threat. But she forgot the sensation in her shoulders as she found herself subjected to the dark fury of his glance. 'The word I used was released, not dismissed and, contrary to what you and my mother thought, my request was made in the hope of having you to myself more often.' He shook her slightly until she fell limply against him. 'Do you have any idea what I've been going through since I was given the news that you'd gone without so much as a word to me?'

She swallowed nervously, realising her mistake. 'I

imagined you would be relieved.'

'Relieved?' he thundered at her, making her flinch.

'Yes, relieved,' she repeated, not quite succeeding in divesting her voice of that note of anguish.

'I feel like throttling you!' he grated harshly, and there was a dangerous look in his incredibly blue eyes when his hands slipped around the back of her neck, his thumbs exerting a pressure in the soft hollows beneath her ears. I've spent the last few days contemplating it,' he added threateningly, 'and it would give me the greatest pleasure now to put my thoughts into action!'

Jennifer wished desperately that she understood the reason for his anger as she managed to whisper, 'Hunter . . . please!'

'You would do well to be afraid, my dear Jennifer,' he warned, easing his hands away from her throat and allowing her to breathe more freely. 'And you can thank your lucky stars that I waited this long before coming here to see you.'

'Why did you come?' she asked hoarsely. 'To insult me for the last time before you finally leave me in peace?'

'I came because I've never wanted another woman the way I want you.'

There it was; direct and to the point, and so typical of Hunter, she thought, a cynical smile curving her soft mouth. 'Were you afraid that you might have missed out on something; something the others had had which I'd denied you?'

'For God's sake, Jennifer!' His eyes blazed down into hers, and he released her at once with a force that made her stagger backwards a pace. 'I don't care about the men in your past; I don't even care about the men in your present. All I want is to be the only man in your future.'

'I'm afraid that's impossible,' she replied, turning away from him with a measure of distaste.

'Why?' he rapped out the question.

'Several reasons,' she snapped, 'and one of them is Carla.'

'Carla is a grasping child playing at being an adult!' he told her harshly, and when she turned slightly to slant a glance up at him, he added savagely, 'She and Stanley have been in love with each other for years, but she imagined it would be more glamorous being mistress of Vogelsvlei, and it amused me to let her think she had a chance. If you must know it all, then I admit that I used her as a barrier against you.'

This disclosure did not surprise Jennifer as much as it might have done had she not suspected something of this nature for quite some time, but the latter part of his statement did have the power to shake her considerably as she discarded Carla mentally to divert their conversation along a different avenue.

'What about Louella?' she asked coldly.

Hunter removed his jacket and flung it across the back of a chair before replying. 'Louella was an acquaintance who put in an untimely appearance. She was the only card I had left eventually, and I played her for all I was worth.'

Jennifer was not quite sure where this conversation was leading, but her glance was accusing as she said: 'You went to her that night when we returned to the hotel.'

'When I left you in the foyer I went to the bar for a stiff whisky before I went up to my room . . . alone,' he explained with a hint of mockery in his voice. 'I telephoned her the next morning to tell her that I'd give her a lift to Plettenberg Bay if she still wanted it, and she accepted.'

'You decided to stay over in Plettenberg Bay because of her,' the words were torn from her lips, and the next moment his hands were heavy on her shoulders, swinging her round to face him, and his ferocious expression made her tremble with a new kind of fear.

'We stayed over in Plettenberg Bay because I'd hoped that, in those surroundings, I would have another opportunity to speak to you, to persuade you, if necessary, that I wouldn't be such a bad proposition, but instead of spending the evening with me, you picked up Dirk Pienaar.'

'I did not pick him up,' she contradicted fiercely. 'We met quite by chance that afternoon when I was on my way down to the beach, and when he asked me to dine with him, I accepted.'

'Jenny,' he began after an angry silence had prevailed, 'let's forget about everyone else, and talk about ourselves for a change.'

Jennifer's mind was in a turmoil. It was gratifying to know that Hunter wanted her despite the murky past he imagined she possessed, but that was not enough for her.

'I'm sorry, Hunter,' she said at last, twisting herself free of his grasp, 'but I can't accept whatever it is you're proposing.'

His eyes narrowed to angry slits once more. 'Why not?'

'Because I don't intend to go to bed with you as your mistress.'

His jaw hardened, and a tiny nerve pulsed against his left temple. She had seen it before, and it was a sure sign that he was furious, or emotionally disturbed, but as that moment she felt almost certain that he was both.

'I'm not asking you to become my mistress, Jennifer,' he replied savagely. 'I'm asking you to become my wife.'

His incredible statement seemed to hover in the air be-

tween them. She was tempted to grasp the offer like a
drowning person grasped at a lifebelt, but there was a part
of her that rejected what he was offering her. He was
offering her marriage merely because he knew he could not
have her any other way, and she was not prepared to accept
that.

'I never thought you would ever go as far as asking a
woman to marry you in your efforts to get what you wanted,'
she remarked in a voice that was heavy with sarcasm, but
she regretted it the next instant when his face became
distorted with fury.

'Damn you, Jennifer! Give me a straight yes or no.'

'No!' she cried hoarsely, refusing him with her lips
while with every part of her being she screamed the
opposite.

He reached for her, but at that moment the doorbell rang,
and she escaped from him to answer it, considering that she
had been lucky so far, but the tension piled higher within
her, for she had no doubt as to the identity of her caller.

'Jennifer, sweetheart!' Mike greeted her with his usual
enthusiasm, pulling her into his arms to plant a friendly
kiss on her cheek. 'You're like a breath of fresh air to a
dying man,' he added dramatically, then his glance went
beyond her towards the man who had been observing them
with smouldering intent, and Mike drew an audible breath
as his arms fell away from her. 'Oh, dear! I seem to have
come at the wrong moment.'

'Come in,' said Jennifer, taking his arm and literally
dragging him inside as some sort of protection. 'The more
the merrier at the moment.'

'I was passing when I saw your light on, so I thought I'd
come up for a chat before going home,' Mike explained, but
Jennifer suspected that his explanation had been directed at

Hunter, and not herself.

She knew that he had come out of concern for her, but Hunter would naturally never believe that.

'Do you make a habit of calling on Jennifer at this late hour for a . . . chat?' Hunter questioned sarcastically, and the atmosphere in her small lounge became electrifying as the two men faced each other.

'Now look here, Hunter, if you'll let me explain——'

'There's no need to explain,' Hunter interrupted Mike harshly, his tight-lipped expression forbidding. 'I understand the situation perfectly, but you may as well know that from this moment onwards Jennifer is no longer available to you. I've asked her to marry me.'

'And I've said no,' Jennifer intervened sharply, her eyes flashing with anger.

'And I don't intend to leave here this evening until she says yes,' Hunter continued as if she had not spoken.

'You have a nerve!' she exclaimed angrily, and Hunter turned abruptly to direct the full fury of his gaze at her.

'I have plenty of nerve, and plenty of time, and you're going to give me the answer I want before I leave here tonight.'

'May I intrude for just a moment?' Mike's voice sliced through the angry silence which had followed Hunter's statement. 'There's one thing you ought to know, Hunter, and, knowing your determination, I'll offer it to you as a wedding present, if you like.'

Hunter turned his glowering glance on Mike. 'The only reason why I'm going to listen is because I like your reference to a wedding present.'

'What I want to say is this,' Mike began before Jennifer had the opportunity to stop him. 'Jennifer and I have known each other for seven years now, and she saw right through me from the start. She's always known me too well to take any amorous advances I may have made seriously, and I've always respected her too much to lure her into bed with me.' Jennifer felt a wave of embarrassing heat sweep up into her face as Mike smiled crookedly and added: 'No one, I'm sure, has had that privilege yet.'

'That's enough, Mike!' she said abruptly, aware of the intensity of Hunter's gaze as it travelled over her, and she turned away from them both to walk towards the window where the cool night air gently brushed against her inflamed cheeks. Tears stung her eyelids, but she blinked them away rapidly, not daring to let them spill over for fear of further humiliation.

'Send me a wedding invitation, will you?' she heard Mike say, and moments later the front door closed behind him.

The silence in the room was strained all at once, and it was broken only by the frightened thudding of her heart. She was afraid of Hunter, but she was more afraid of herself, and she was aware of him now with every fibre of her being as he approached her. She felt the heat of his body against her back, and then his hands were on her shoulders, turning her to face him. Her eyes were defiant when they met his, but it was the hard, unrelenting line of his jaw that made her realise exactly what she was up against. His thumbs moved against the sensitive hollows at the base of her throat where her pulse was beating fast and erratic, and his sensual touch was arousing emotions she was finding desperately hard to suppress.

'Jenny . . .'

'You're wasting your time,' she said jerkily.

'I love you.'

'I don't care! I'm not going to——' His words penetrated

at last, leaving her to wonder incredulously whether she had suddenly gone quite mad. 'What did you say?' she asked in no more than a hoarse whisper.

'I want you, I need you, I love you, and I'm damned if I'm going to let you go until you say you'll marry me,' he elaborated harshly, his hands no longer caressing, but almost rough against her shoulders as he dragged her against him with a fierceness that was a sweet agony. 'You tore the heart out of me that first day we met,' he blazed down at her, 'and since then I've had to fight every inch of the way for my existence. You've frustrated and infuriated me; and I've spent most of my days and nights in a jealous rage, wanting you, yet damned if I would share you. I've hated myself, and I've hated you, but these last few days at Vogelsvlei without you have been sheer hell.'

The most exquisite happiness surged through her, warming her chilled heart, and lighting a glow within her that spread to her eyes. 'Hunter . . .'

'You've become the essence of my life, Jenny,' he continued as if she had not spoken, 'and it took these past few days without you to make me realise that, no matter what you are, or what you've been, my life would be worthless without you.'

'Don't say any more . . . please,' she begged, his tortured expression wrenching at her heart. 'I'm to blame for many of the opinions you formed of me, but there's one thing you must believe.' The colour deepened in her cheeks, but she withstood the probing intensity of his eyes. 'I've never slept with a man before,' she said unsteadily. 'Never, Hunter. Not even once.'

'God, Jennifer,' he groaned, and there was something close to remorse in the way he looked at her that told her he believed her, and, tightening his arms about her, he buried his face against her pulsating throat. 'I owe you an apology, and I don't quite know where to begin.'

'Hush!' she whispered urgently, finding it oddly disquieting to see him humbled in this manner, and slipping her arms about his waist, she pressed closer to him and said the words she had whispered so many times before into the darkness of her lonely room. 'I love you, Hunter.'

He raised his head and, for the first time, she held his glance without hiding what was in her heart. His eyes, too, were saying the most incredibly wonderful things.

'Do you love me enough to marry me?' he asked.

'Yes,' she replied without further hesitation.

She slid her hands upwards across his back towards his shoulders, and felt the muscles ripple and harden beneath her touch. His deep blue eyes were almost black now with the intensity of his emotions, and then his mouth was ravaging her willing lips, plundering their softness with a hunger that matched her own. Their arms tightened about each other, as if they could not bear to let anything come between them, until desire, sharp and sweet, made them draw a little apart. Jennifer's face was flushed, and her eyes glowed with a happiness she knew she could never put into words, but one look at her was enough to make Hunter draw a sharp breath before he moulded her to the hard length of his body once more. It was a long time before he released her again, and this time she was not only flushed, but breathless and trembling with the force of the emotions he had aroused within her.

'I almost forgot,' he said, moving away from her towards the large flat box he had flung so angrily into a chair on his arrival. 'I have something for you.'

The box exchanged hands, and while she undid the wrapping Hunter eased his great length on to her small

sofa and watched her from beneath lowered lids with a
faint smile playing about his hard mouth.

Jennifer finally lifted the lid and carefully removed the
layer of tissue paper. What she saw made her heart leap
wildly into her throat, and her hands were shaking almost
uncontrollably when she lifted out the ostrich feather cape
and held it up before her. It was made from the white plume
feathers of the male ostrich, but what caught her enchanted
attention were the spotted plumes which had been sewn
in to form a perfect border around the outer edge of the
magnificent cape.

'Oh, Hunter, it's beautiful!' she whispered, her heart too
full to say much more as she ran her hands lightly and
caressingly over the soft feathers.

'This is another reason why I waited so long before coming here to see you,' he explained. 'Danny's wife is pretty
good with this sort of thing, and she hadn't finished it yet
when you left so unexpectedly, but I practically had her
working round the clock these last few days to complete
it for you.'

Jennifer went weak with love for him. 'Do you know
what Agnes said when she saw these spotted plumes?' she
asked, and when he shook his head she said: 'She claimed
it was a sign that you would be married before the end
of this year, and it seems that she was right after all.'

'*Damn* right!' Hunter agreed, his glittering glance
travelling over her with a certain intimacy which set her
nerves quivering responsively. 'Come here, woman. I
want you.'

He gave her no opportunity to refuse. His fingers latched
on to her wrist, and she was pulled down roughly on to the
sofa beside him. His mouth came down on to hers before
she had time to draw breath, and her lips were not unwilling

when he brushed them apart with his. With his body he forced her into the corner of the sofa, and then his hands were travelling over her in a sensual caress that did not fail to arouse her. His fingers pulled the pins from her hair, and when it cascaded down on to her shoulders he buried his face in its fragrant silkiness.

'I have instructions to take you back to Vogelsvlei with me tomorrow,' he finally told her, his lips moving warm and urgently against her throat where her pulse was throbbing with primitive haste.

'It seems to me your mother was very sure you would succeed in your quest,' she murmured unsteadily, running her hands lovingly over his crisp, dark hair until her fingers came to rest against the back of his strong neck.

'I was practically ordered not to return if I failed.'

Jennifer laughed softly. 'I can almost believe that, but what about my job?'

'It took a little persuasion, but my aunt, in her capacity as Matron, has agreed to sign your release papers,' he said, and this explained Matron Griffiths' reluctance to see her that morning.

'You've obviously thought of everything.'

'When I want something badly enough, I make sure that nothing stands in my way,' he murmured against her lips. 'And I happen to want you.'

Her lips parted beneath his, and excitement churned through her, making her unaware of those strong brown fingers undoing the buttons of her blouse. The front catch of her bra offered the least resistance, and it was only when she felt the urgent, caressing pressure of his large hands against her breasts that she realised what he had done. It was too late then to protest, for her breasts were swelling in response to his touch, and desire was like a fiery flame igniting all her natural instincts. Her hands moved of their own volition, her fingers tugging impatiently at the buttons of his shirt until her palms made contact with his hard, hair-roughened chest. She could feel his heart beating as wildly as her own, but her hands stilled their caresses when she realised that her innocent longing to touch him had quickened his own desire to possess her.

'Are you going to let me stay the night?' he asked thickly, his lips tantalising hers until she almost cried out with the need for his kisses.

She wanted him very much, but not like this. It was important to her to come to her husband on their wedding night untouched even by him, and it was important that she have Hunter's respect as well as his love.

'Don't make it difficult for me to—to refuse you,' she begged at last.

'You don't know how tempted I am to do just that.'

'I know,' she breathed, clinging desperately now to her sanity as he lowered his lips to her smooth, satiny breast. 'I—I love you more than I could ever tell you, but I—I also happen to be terribly old-fashioned,' she added unsteadily, a little afraid now as she felt her body yield beneath the sensual insistence of his lips and hands.

'You're not going to make me wait long, are you?' he growled, raising his head to glare down at her in that old ferocious manner, but this time it did not frighten her, and a provocative little smile curved her generous mouth.

'It would be in my own interests not to, I think,' she replied softly, her eyes luminous with love as she traced the line of his hard jaw with tender, teasing fingers.

'You're damn right about that!' he snapped harshly, but there was an unexpected look of tenderness in his eyes, and then she was subjected to another bout of lovemaking that left her quivering on the brink of desire.

His arms were strong yet gentle about her, and with the first throes of hunger assuaged, his kisses became tender, yet lingering with the warmth of suppressed passion. He did not try to make her change her mind about letting him stay the night with her and, knowing how much he wanted her, she admired him for his control. He knew, too, how much she wanted him—she had not hidden the fact—but he respected her wishes, and she knew that she would have no need to fear that he would make demands on her until they could give of each other freely on their wedding night.

When Hunter finally left her flat that evening she sat for a long time staring at the cape he had given her with the spotted plumes worked into it, and running her fingers over it lightly she decided that they had brought her good fortune. She had won the love of the often rude, arrogant master of Vogelsvlei, and all that remained was for her to win his complete trust. She was indeed fortunate, she realised, and it was with a light, happy heart that she went to bed that night. Soon, very soon, she would be Hunter's wife, and her impossible dreams would become a beautiful reality.

Harlequin Plus

A WORD ABOUT THE AUTHOR

Yvonne Whittal grew up in South Africa, spending her summers on the coast and her winter months inland at a sheep farm in the Karoo region. It was there that Yvonne came to know the farmers who loved the earth and faced a never ending struggle for survival. Her first novel, *East to Barryvale* (Romance #1915, published in 1975), was inspired by the people of the area.

Yvonne began scribbling stories at a very early age, and in her teens she considered writing as a profession. But marriage and three daughters caused her to shelve that idea...for a while.

Then, rusty after so many years away from her writing, Yvonne enrolled in a fiction-writing course and set to work. She began with short stories and moved on to a novel, which took several months to complete. "Fortunately," she laughingly comments on her slow start, "I did not have to make a living out of my writing then. Otherwise, I would surely have starved!"

FREE!
Romance Treasury

**A beautifully bound,
value-packed,
three-in-one
volume of romance!**

FREE!

A hardcover Romance Treasury volume
containing 3 treasured works of romance
by 3 outstanding Harlequin authors...

...as your introduction to Harlequin's
Romance Treasury subscription plan!

Romance Treasury

...almost 600 pages of exciting romance reading
every month at the low cost of $6.97 a volume!

A wonderful way to collect many of Harlequin's most beautiful love
stories, all originally published in the late '60s and early '70s.
Each value-packed volume, bound in a distinctive gold-embossed
leatherette case and wrapped in a colorfully illustrated dust jacket,
contains...
• 3 full-length novels by 3 world-famous authors of romance fiction
• a unique illustration for every novel
• the elegant touch of a delicate bound-in ribbon bookmark...
  and much, much more!

Romance Treasury

...for a library of romance you'll treasure forever!

Complete and mail today the FREE gift certificate and subscription
reservation on the following page.

Romance Treasury

An exciting opportunity to collect treasured works of romance! Almost 600 pages of exciting romance reading in each beautifully bound hardcover volume!

You may cancel your subscription whenever you wish! You don't have to buy any minimum number of volumes. Whenever you decide to stop your subscription just drop us a line and we'll cancel all further shipments.